A TRUTHFUL KISS

(SIGNED WITH A KISS, BOOK 3)

JESSICA SORENSEN

1

ALEXIS

I'M LEANING *over him as he lies on the cracked tile floor. I push him down, ignoring his silent cries for help.*

"I'm sorry," I tell him as I hold his face against the floor, "but I have to do this."

"Please," he begs in desperation.

My chest tightens. I don't want to do this. Wish I couldn't, but

…

"I'm sorry," I whisper. "But either you have to shatter, or I do."

Then I break him apart, bit by bit, peeling away his layers until I reach his heart.

Then I shatter it.

Shatter West's heart.

And he doesn't cry.

He doesn't scream.

No, he's quiet.

Almost like he died—

My eyelids snap open as my alarm blares. Blinking several times against the soft sunlight of the sunrise slipping through the blinds on my bedroom window, I roll over, pick up my phone, and turn the alarm off.

Normally, I'd go back to sleep, wake up a half an hour later, and be tardy for school. Today, I'm wide awake, thoughts of what happened over spring break plaguing my mind. Thoughts of my blackmailer plaguing my mind.

Really, after what happened yesterday, I'm surprised I even managed to fall asleep at all. The blackmailer had informed me of what they wanted me to do. They also showed me just how dangerous they could be.

They cut my battery cable and threatened to cut my brake cables next time.

They snuck into my house and stole my mom's locket.

They snuck into West's temporary house and watched me sleep.

They have videos of me graffitiing places across town. And they have videos of that day. That fucking day that nearly destroyed me almost the same way as I was going to destroy West in the dream I just had.

I'm well aware of why I had the dream. Because the blackmailer wants me to destroy West. Or, well, break his heart. But that doesn't make any sense to me. How can I break his heart when he's not in love with me? According to the blackmailer, though, he is.

Could he be?

I roll my eyes as the ludicrous thought briefly crosses my mind. Up until a few days ago, West and I have been frenemies. West is in no way, shape, or form in love with me. This is just the blackmailers way of getting into my head, something they're succeeding at. And they're doing this because they want revenge for me taking away their fun. At least, that's what they said. That doesn't help me pinpoint who they are, since I'm sure a lot of people want revenge.

"Dammit," I breathe aloud. At the moment, I'm kind of regretting some of my life choices.

Alexis Baker, dwelling on her life choices? Man, this stuff must really be messing with my mind. I need to focus on something else, like dragging my ass out of bed and getting ready for school. Even though I have no desire to go. Honestly, part of me is really considering ditching. But Loki would freak out if I did. Plus, I might be giving the blackmailer more stuff to hold against me if I do.

Control.

Until I figure out who they are, they can control me. I hate being controlled. Both the old Alexis and the new one does.

I need to figure out who they are as quickly as possible.

Sitting up in the bed, I throw the blankets off and pick up my phone from off the nightstand. Then I dial West's number to see if, by chance, Ellis has figured out who's been texting me all the threatening text and videos.

"Hey," he answers after three rings. He sounds a little bit better than he did yesterday. "I was just about to call you."

I perk up, wondering if he was because he has information. "Really?"

"Yeah. I was heading out of the house to go meet my mom, and I … well, I just wanted to talk to you before I go."

"Okay, what about?"

"Nothing really. I'm just not looking forward to seeing her. At all. And talking to you seems to cheer me up."

"Really?" I ask with a hint of doubt in my tone.

"Yes, really." I can hear the smile in his voice. "Although, I'm still feeling a bit down. Maybe I should come over, and you can give me another hug. Now that might cheer me up a fucking ton."

I roll my eyes, even though he can't see me. "I only did that because you seemed super sad."

"I'm super sad now. In fact, I'm the saddest I've ever been." But the hint of amusement in his tone suggests otherwise.

"You don't sound sad at all," I point out, standing up and stretching my arm above my head.

"Well, I am," he assures me. "I'm so sad that I think the only thing that'll cheer me up is a hug from you. No, I changed my mind. I think a kiss is the only thing that'll work."

Okay, he definitely sounds better than he did yesterday. Why, though? Did something happen that cheered him up? Did his mom inform him she was lying about him being adopted?

I glance at the photo I sketched of him yesterday. After I finished, I hung it on my wall as a reminder of why I need to get over my issues, at least some, and be there for West like he's been there for me.

But that doesn't mean kissing him.

Friends. We need to just be friends. Well, at least in real life. In pretend, fake dating land, I know I'm going to have to kiss him. But right now …

"I'm not going to kiss you." As the words leave my lips, I can almost feel his lips brushing against mine.

"Okay." He sounds about as doubtful as I feel.

"Whatever," I say with a roll of my eyes. "If you just called to flirt, I'm going to hang up, because I need to get ready for school, or else I'm going to be late."

He snickers into the phone. "Alexis Baker worried about being late for school. Now that's a new one."

"Dude, you're so asking for it."

"Aw, please don't tease me like that."

My heart flutters in my chest, but I tell it to shut the hell up. That we're so not doing this. That we can't even do it, considering what's going on with this whole blackmailer situation.

Speaking of which, should I tell him what happened?

The blackmailer said not to, but I don't know … How would they even know?

"Okay, I'm hanging up," I tell him then move to end the call.

"Lex, I'm just messing with you," he hurriedly says. "I'll stop. Just don't hang up yet."

"Why not?" I ask, wondering why he seems so determined to keep me on the phone.

"Because … I'm heading to talk to my mom and … I don't know … I just need someone to talk to." The humor is slowly seeping out from his tone.

My heart aches for him as I remember what he found out yesterday, about how he may have been adopted.

"Are you going to ask your mom about what you found out yesterday?" I tread cautiously.

"Yeah. That's basically the only reason why I'm going. I want to find out if she was telling the truth."

"And what if she was?"

"Then at least I can cut ties with her and my dad … Or the man who raised me, I guess."

"West, I'm sorry." I'm unsure of what else to say.

"It's fine. It's not your fault."

"I know, but I still feel bad." I sigh. "Is there anything I can do to help?"

Silence stretches between us. He clearly wants to ask me something, but what?

"Actually, I need to talk to you about something," he

says. "Can you maybe go with me somewhere at lunchtime?"

Normally, there'd be no way I'd go to lunch with West, but a lot has changed over the course of a week. Plus, we're technically supposed to be fake dating.

"Yeah, sure," I reply. "Honestly, we should probably have lunch, anyway, since we're technically supposed to be dating."

"True," he agrees. "All right then, I'll meet you at your locker after fourth period. It can be our first official date."

"Fake date," I correct.

"Mmmhmm," is all he says. I start to ask what he means by that when he adds, "Crap. I'm here. That was a shorter drive than I wanted. I gotta go."

"Okay." I prepare to hang up, but it feels like something else needs to be said. "If you need anything, text me, okay? I keep my phone on me in class, even though we're not supposed to."

"You little rebel," he teases.

I shake my head, throwing back at him, "Like you're one to talk."

He laughs. "I guess we're perfect for each other." Before I can ream into him for that, he says, "Bye, Lex. Talk to you soon."

We hang up then and, for a moment, I just sit there, highly aware of how light I feel after talking to him. I'm not sure what that means, but I feel like it might mean something, which really freaks me out for a lot of reasons.

It has me worried. Not just that I'm starting to feel things for West, but that because, starting today, I have to start making West fall in love with me so I can break his heart.

What if I break both of ours in the process?

My stomach churns at the thought. And that churning sensation only magnifies when I receive a text from the blackmailer.

Unknown: Are you ready to start the game?

"What damn game?" I mutter, hovering my fingers over the keyboard as I deliberate what to say.

Me: You keep saying we're playing a game, but how am I supposed to know how to play if I don't even know what game I'm playing?

Unknown: That'll be revealed in time. Right now, the rules are pretty simple: do what I say and no one will get hurt.

I swallow the lump wedged in my throat. Maybe I should just tell the police; let myself deal with the consequences.

Unknown: Oh yeah, and as an added enticement, I thought I'd throw this in there. Your brother is currently under scrutiny by CPS. If you don't want a ton of child neglect reports to flow in, I'd recommend doing what I say.

Anger burns underneath my skin. How dare he bring my family into this? How dare he threaten them?

Me: Don't you dare bring my family into this.

Unknown: I won't as long as you do what I say.

The muscles in my jaw pulsate as I reread the messages. It dawns on me then that this is evidence. Evidence that I can prove I've been blackmailed.

I need to tell Loki.

Swallowing hard, I make my way down the stairs where Loki is pouring a cup of coffee. He's dressed in a button-down shirt and pants—his work clothes.

"Don't forget that you're supposed to paint the store after school today," he tells me as he sets the coffee pot down. "And then, this weekend, I want you to help out at the store."

"Okay." I take a deep breath and step farther into the kitchen. *You can do this. You can do this. You can do this.* "Loki, there's something I need to tell you."

He glances up at me with a frown on his face. "What happened?"

I hate that he thinks something happened, but I guess it kind of did.

This is all my fault. If I'd just stayed out of trouble, then the blackmailer wouldn't have all this dirt on me.

"I've been getting these messages." I swipe my finger across the screen of my phone and move to open the messages. Then my heart nearly bottoms into my stomach.

They're gone. The entire thread.

"No, no, no, no, no," I mutter under my breath as panic flares through me.

This isn't happening. This can't be happening. But, as I stare down at my screen, I realize that, yes, this is happening. That either I somehow deleted the thread or the black-mailer did.

"Nothing. Never mind," I tell Loki as I back out of the kitchen.

He looks at me with concern. "Lex, are you okay?"

"Yep." I plaster on the fakest smile ever then whirl around and rush out of the kitchen, panic soaring through me.

When I reach my room, I shut the door and let out a shaky breath. Who is this person doing this to me?

"God, I hope West finds out something soon," I mumble.

Until then, I guess I'll play the game.

Or at least pretend to, something I'm unfortunately good at.

2

WEST

IF I DIDN'T NEED answers, I wouldn't be here. I'm exhausted, slightly hungover, and have a lot of other stuff to worry about, like figuring out how Blaine is attached to this blackmailing thing with Alexis, and figuring out what I'm going to do about what Jay did to Alexis. Because I'm going to do something. Killing him was the first thing that came to mind, but I don't think I'm a killer. I'm definitely up for tormenting, though. I just need a plan.

First, I need to focus on getting through breakfast with my parents. That's the thing, though. They might not be my parents. But this is the only way to get to the bottom of if they are, who they are to me, why they adopted me if they clearly hate kids, and who in the hell are my real parents.

Sucking in a deep breath, I climb out of the car then

head inside one of the few five-star hotels in Honeyton. It has a restaurant attached to it that serves bottomless mimosas, which is why I'm assuming we're here—my fake mother has a thing for mimosas. And wine. And pills.

When I peer in the restaurant area, though, I can't spot them anywhere, so I dig out my phone and send Loraine, aka my questionable mother, a text.

Me: Where are you? I'm by the restaurant, and you're not there.

Loraine: We're not meeting at the restaurant. We're meeting in one of the rooms. Take the elevator to the six floor and go to room 618.

"What the hell is she up to?" I mutter as I make my way past the front desk and toward the elevators.

The receptionist behind the desk scrutinizes me as I pass, her gaze scrolling over my nearly all-black outfit, my unlaced boots, my facial piercings, and my bloodshot eyes.

I used to not look like this. I used to dress preppy like my parents wanted me to. It's crazy because I'm the same person I've always been, yet put on some nice clothes and people treat you differently, like you're a better person if you look put together on the outside.

That's a bunch of bullshit. My parents are proof of that. They're two of the most put together people on the outside. On the inside, though, monsters live; one full of rage and anger, the other numb, cold, and uncaring.

And I'm about to go face those monsters head-on.

"Can I help you?" the receptionist calls out.

"Nope," I throw back at her.

She narrows her eyes at me. "If you don't have a room here, you can't be here. And if you don't leave, I'll call security."

Grinding my teeth, I spin around and approach the desk. "I don't have a room, sweetheart," I say, my tone oozing annoyance. "But my parents do. You might know them. They're Loraine and Eli Averson."

Her expression immediately falls. "How do you know the Aversons?"

"Like I said, they're my parents."

She swallows audibly. "Oh. I didn't know."

"Well, now you do." I pat the counter then walk off, leaving her to think I'm going to tattle on her rude behavior. Like if I did, my parents would care enough to get her in trouble. They don't. If I told them what happened, they'd get pissed off at me for being dressed the way I am now.

Once I make my way out of the lobby, I take the elevator up to the sixth floor and find the room. I pause in front of it, taking a collective breath before knocking. I know I need to keep my shit together, but nervousness jitters through me. I wish I was stronger than this, but I'm not. At least not with my parents. And I'm really fucking worried about what my mom is going to tell me.

My nervousness only grows when my mom opens the

door. She's tipsy—that much I can tell—her eyes a bit glassy, and her breath reeks of wine.

And I thought I was bad.

Still, despite the fact that she's drunk, she appears as put together as she always does, not a wrinkle in her dress, her hair perfectly curled.

Always look perfect, she used to tell me. *Even if you aren't.*

She eyes me over with eyes that I suddenly realize look nothing like mine. Then she frowns and shakes her head, stepping back into the room. "You can come in."

Sighing, I step over the threshold and shut the door behind me. Then I walk into the room. Or, well, suite. The bed is made and, other than the wine and empty plates on the table, there's no sign she's been staying in this room, which leaves me wondering … "Why are we meeting in a hotel room?" I ask as I stand in the middle of the room, on edge.

Something is off. I can feel it.

"To avoid the risk of this conversation ever being over-heard." She makes her way over to a table near the large windows in the far corner of the room and takes a seat. "Sit down. We need to talk."

Wariness floods my body. I don't budge. "What about?"

She narrows her eyes at me, her lips parting, but she's cut off by the sound of the toilet flushing.

I tense, my gaze darting to the bathroom door as it

opens. When my father walks out, I'm not sure whether to be relieved or get even more tense.

"These towels here are like sandpaper," he says as he tosses the hand towel that he's drying his hands off with onto the bathroom counter. "Honeyton is really going downhill ..." He trails off when he notices me standing there. His entire face shifts then, going from casual to hard in the matter of a second, but he usually looks at me this way. "So, you're here."

I shrug, stuffing my hands into the pockets of my jeans to hide my uneasiness. "I was told to be, wasn't I? Well, more like threatened into coming here." It's a bold move to say that to him.

Unlike with my mom, my dad is a lot harder to stand up to. But I'm tired. Fucking exhausted. Have been for years now, and things are only getting worse, something I was reminded of last night when I helped Holden and Ellis deal drugs to some rich assholes.

"Yeah, well, sometimes threatening is the only thing that can get through that thick head of yours," my father responds in a cold tone. "Well, that and a good beating."

The muscles in my jaw pulsate. I want to hit him. So badly. Have for the longest time. But I know where that'll lead. And no, I'm not talking about getting arrested. That's not my dad's style. Too many people would find out. No, he'd handle it a bit differently, probably by hitting me back and then some. Maybe it'd be worth it. Maybe getting beat would be worth that swing I'd get in, that satisfaction of knowing that, for once, *I* hurt *him*.

"West, get that look off your face and come sit down," my mom orders in an uneven tone, like she knows exactly what my thoughts are.

I stare at my father for a slamming heartbeat longer, and he stares right back, daring me.

My fingers twitch to do it, to hit him like I hit Blaine.

"Go ahead," my father dares, stepping toward me. "See what happens."

"That's enough," my mom hisses. "If you two start fighting in here, someone could overhear and call the police. And then you'll never be elected."

My father grinds his teeth while carrying my gaze. He doesn't want to be the first one to look away. Neither do I.

"Fine, you want to be the tough guy, then go ahead," he murmurs, glaring at me. "I'll be the adult here."

As he looks away, I get this twisted sense of satisfaction over it.

I fucking defied him, and it felt so damn good.

That feeling is quickly extinguished when I sit down at the table and my mom informs me of why she brought me here.

"We need you to sign these papers," she says as she opens a folder. "Your dad is a notary, so we don't need anyone else present." She shoves a pen at me.

I take the pen from her and confusedly stare down at

the papers as she slides the folder in my direction. "What are these?"

"That's not for you to worry about," she tells me in a curt tone. "Just sign the papers, and then you can go."

I'm so beyond confused.

"But I thought you …" I glance at her, unable to get the words out.

I thought I was adopted. I thought that's why you brought me here. To talk about it.

"You thought I what?" She plays dumb, but I can tell she knows what I mean.

My father moves up behind me and leans over my shoulder. "Just sign the damn papers, you fucking idiot," he says in a low tone then grabs my hand and tries to force me to do so.

A while ago, I might have, but I think I've reached my breaking point.

I jerk back, jumping to my feet, which makes my dad stumble back as my chair topples over.

"What the fuck is wrong with you?" he growls out, his face bright red.

"I'm not just going to sign some damn papers because you guys said so." I pick up the papers. "When I read them over, I'll decide if I will sign them."

I've never seen him as livid as he looks in that moment, his face red with anger, his eyes dark and full of warning that he's about to break me. But this time, I'm not going to let him.

I dodge around him with the papers in my hand. He tries to grab me, but I shove him away, and he's so shocked by the move that it takes him a moment to recover, which gives me enough time to run out of the room.

Since the hallway is empty, he chases after me. I run, heading for the stairs instead of the elevator since I'd have to wait for it.

"West," he growls out as he sprints after me.

But I'm faster than him and reach the stairs before he can get to me. As I haul ass down the stairway, he chases me for a bit. When I reach the bottom floor, though, and exit the stairwell, he stops, probably knowing that if he continues to chase me, people are going to see him.

I powerwalk through the lobby, ignoring the receptionist as she tries to apologize for earlier. When I burst out the front doors, I jog for my car and climb in. Then I start the engine, and my tires spin as I peel out of the parking lot.

Even though I want to look at the papers first, I know I need to go, because I wouldn't put it past my parents—whoever the hell they are—to try to corner me while I'm in my car.

I drive for several minutes, my heart racing in my chest, my phone vibrating with incoming messages that I'm sure are from Loraine and Eli. I ignore them, trying to process what I just did.

I'm so damn screwed. I know this, and while part of me cares, part of me doesn't. I just want to be done with them and their games. But I'm not done yet. No. I need to see what's on those papers, see why they seemed so desperate for me to sign them.

Flipping on my blinker, I make a turn into the parking lot of the local grocery store. Then I park near the front doors where a lot of people are going in and out, so if my parents do spot my car and try to confront me, enough people will be around that they won't make a scene.

I put the shifter into park and leave the engine idling in case I need to take off. Then I pick up the folder and start to skim-read the papers. They're clearly some sort of legal documents, and while I can't understand all of it, I get the basic gist of what they contain.

Someone has left me a large sum of money in their will, and signing these papers will basically transfer all the money over to my parents. But the question is: who left me the money? Why? And why do my parents need the money so badly when they already have enough as it is?

I may not be able to find most of those answers right now, but I can find one.

I flip through the papers, searching for a name. It takes me a moment to find it.

Charlotte Everlyson.

"Who are you?" I mutter. "And why did you leave me so much money?"

A couple of ideas come to mind, like maybe this Charlotte was my real mother. But, if that's true, then that means what Loraine said about me being adopted is true.

It also means that my real mother is dead.

3

ALEXIS

BEFORE I LEAVE FOR SCHOOL, I check under the hood and do a brake check to make sure everything is good with my car. I feel extremely paranoid, but after everything that's happened, I think that might be justifiable.

Once I'm certain my car is good, I hop in and make the drive to school.

During the drive, my mind is plagued by thoughts of this blackmailer and how in the hell they got so good with electronics. Clearly, they have to be some sort of hacker, which has me extremely worried.

While I don't know a ton about hacking, I've read enough to understand that a hacker may be able to access a lot of information about me. And they broke into my house, too, which shows they're not afraid to break the law. I just wish I knew why they were doing this. Knew why they believed I'd done something to them. They mentioned it once in a text, that I ruined their life.

That honestly doesn't give me a clue as to who it could be. The really sucky part is the list of people who would want to torment me is pretty long. Although, I don't really know anyone who has awesome hacking skills. In fact, if I was to go by that, it'd eliminate every suspect I can think of. However, any of these suspects could be getting help from a hacker. I mean, look at West. He knew Ellis, who is a hacker, and is using him to figure out who is sending me the texts.

If he can't figure out who the sender is, what the heck am I supposed to do? They already erased the thread of texts they sent me, which really is the only evidence I have against them.

What I need is a game plan, a way to figure out who this is and gather some evidence against them.

Yeah, that could work. At least, it works in the mystery books I read.

When I arrive at the school parking lot, I find a place to park. Then I dig out a notebook and pen out of my backpack, figuring I'll go old-school with this instead of making a list on the note app in my phone. That way, the list can't be hacked into.

At the top of the page I write: *My To-do List:*

Below it, I scribble a short list.

1. *Find out who's texting me.*
2. *Find out why.*
3. *Find out dirt on them.*
4. *Use it against them to get them to stop blackmailing me.*
5. *Find a way to delete that video of you.*

The list is pretty vague, but I'll add more detail to it once I learn more.

Closing the notebook, I tuck it away in my bag then grab my keys and get out of the car, feeling a little bit better. However, it's a short-lived feeling as school starts and reminds me of other problems I haven't yet dealt with.

I was really distracted over the weekend and didn't think too much about it. About how I'd see Masie and wouldn't be able to just take off and avoid her. I didn't think about how I'd have to see Masie and Blaine, holding hands and looking into each other's eyes, all lovey-dovey. I also didn't think about how many people would be gushing over how cute of a couple they make.

"Oh my God, they're so cute together," Jane, one of the biggest gossiper in school, gushes to her friend Stella as she's walking out of third period.

The two of them are in front of me, lollygagging down the aisle, taking their sweet-ass time and blocking my path.

"Blaine and Masie?" Stella asks as she texts on her phone.

"Um, duh. Who else would I be talking about?" Jane rolls her eyes as they continue to lollygag toward the door, blocking my way. "It's all anyone is talking about."

No, it's not. It's all *she's* talking about. Everyone else acts like they expected it to happen. Or they already knew about Masie and Blaine's relationship, which makes me wonder if they already did.

Was I the only one who was blindsided?

I shake my head at myself, wondering if I've just been seeing what I've wanted to see.

I must have.

"Yeah …" Stella is really distracted by her phone, and it's making her walk slow as hell.

I hug my books against my chest, telling myself to be patient, but not only is their what has to be an attempt to break the world's slowest walking record getting on my nerves, so is their topic of conversation.

The reason behind my irritation toward the subject of Masie and Blaine isn't what I thought it would be. I thought I'd be jealous, but I'm kind of just pissed off. Pissed off that my two best friends lied to me, had secret conversations behind my back about my crush on Blaine. I feel like I just discovered who they both are, and my feelings for Blaine dissolved along with my friendship with Masie.

Not that she hasn't been trying to fix our friendship. She tried to corner me this morning before school started, but I stealthy ducked into class. I haven't seen her since then, but I think I may have just spotted her outside of the classroom.

"I thought you had a thing for Blaine?" Stella asks Jane as she continues to text on her phone.

"That was so forever ago. Now I'm totally after Jay," she declares. "He is so, so hot. And I heard he's supposed to be going to the lake party this weekend. We should go."

Every single part of me locks up at the mention of Jay. I want to scream at her, tell her what a piece of shit he is, but the words become thick in my throat.

"Maybe." Stella stuffs her phone into the back pocket of her jeans. "You think West will be there?"

And now my stomach is winding into knots. Wait—West? As in, *my* West?

Well, he's not really mine. We're just pretending, and Stella doesn't know about my and West's fake relationship yet, so why am I getting all worked up? I shouldn't care at all. But I do. In fact, I've been worried about West all morning. Not that I've heard from him. Maybe that's a good sign. Maybe that means everything went smoothly this morning. But, how can finding out you're adopted go smoothly, especially with how his mother told him?

Yeah, there's no way things went smoothly.

Then, where is he?

Maybe I should just text him.

I'm debating if I should when Jane and Stella finally, finally reach the door. They turn right, heading down the hallway away from me and taking their conversation that has veered toward how delicious West's lips look with them.

I breathe in relief and head to the left toward my locker, making it a whole three steps before Masie steps out of the crowd and in front of me.

So, it was her I saw. Crap.

"I don't want to talk to you," I say before she can even get a word out.

She looks at me like a wounded deer. "Lex, please. We need to talk. I don't want this one little thing to ruin our friendship."

Little thing? She may think that's what it is, but she hurt me in ways I'll never be able to tell her aloud.

I lower my voice as people turn to look at us. "I said I don't want to talk about it." I move to step around her, but she skitters in front of me again, nearly tripping in her heels.

If I wanted to, I could just take off and outrun her. Masie can't run for shit. Plus, she's wearing a dress and heels while I have on shorts, clunky boots, and a black tank top, all of which are easy to run in. Well, they would be except I think my laces are untied. Then again, I spent all weekend running from her, and I'm getting tired of it.

"Move out of my way," I warn, crossing my arms and staring her down.

"No," she replies, her tone a little shaky. "Not until you talk to me."

I shake my head, my jaw ticking. "I don't owe you anything. You're the one that backstabbed me, not the other way around."

"I didn't backstab you," she says, her eyes watering up. "I just fell for Blaine. I didn't mean to. It just happened. And I tried to fight my feelings for him for a long time, because I knew you loved him, but it's like we were meant for each other, Lex." A tear rolls down her cheek, but she quickly wipes it away with her hand. "I think I'm in love with him, Lex."

Maybe if she'd told me this beforehand, things might've been different. Or maybe if she hadn't just declared to everyone in the hallway that I had feelings for Blaine, I would have felt sorry for her.

As the whispering and staring starts to spread like a freakin' zombie plague, my heart rate picks up, thudding deafeningly inside my chest.

Everyone knows. This is what you were afraid of.

Say something, Alexis. Do anything.

I suddenly become that girl on the bathroom floor again, the freak who people made fun of. I start to shrink inside myself.

I should run. Run home and grab a can of spray paint so I can distract myself from anything else other than this moment. And maybe I would've done just that if West hadn't shown up at that precise moment.

"Hey," he greets me, sliding his arm around my lower back as he moves up beside me.

I'm about to say "hey" back, am about to melt into him even if it makes me seem weak, when he does something completely unexpected.

He presses his lips to mine.

The kiss doesn't last long, but it's enough to send my already racing heart skyrocketing. When he pulls back, the corners of his lips quirk with amusement, though his eyes look a bit wild, like he just surprised the hell out of himself almost as much as he did me.

"What the hell is happening right now?" Masie breathes out, wide-eyed, gaze flicking between West and me.

"Hey, Masie?" West says to her curtly.

"Yeah?" she asks, confusion flooding her eyes.

West rests his hand on the small of my back as he looks at her. "Get the fuck out of my way so I can walk my girlfriend to class."

She blinks. "Girlfriend?" Her gaze lands on me, and she has the audacity to look hurt. "You're dating West, and you didn't tell me?"

Guilt wells in my throat, and it pisses me off. I shouldn't care. At all. But I do a little bit, which is annoying. I pretend it's not that way at all.

I arch my brow at her. "It hurts, doesn't it? Knowing that your best friend kept this huge secret from you."

Her expression falls, and her lips part.

West steers me around her before she can get a word out. Then we walk down the crowded hallway, not really saying anything, mostly because everyone is watching us.

I expect him to walk me to my next class, but he passes by the classroom. That's when I realize West probably has no clue what my next class is.

"Um, we passed my class," I tell him, starting to slow down.

"I know," he tells me. "I need to talk to you for a minute. You might be a little late." He glances at me, amusement glittering in his eyes. "You okay with being a little bit tardy, Alexis the Rebellious?"

"No." I snort a laugh. "And FYI, that's a dumbass nickname."

"Noted. I'll think of something better." He grins at me. "Like a good boyfriend would."

I roll my eyes again, but I'm on the verge of smiling.

Of course, that smile morphs into confusion as he leads me outside of the school.

"Where are we going?" I wonder as he removes his hand from my lower back.

I assume he does it since we're outdoors where no one is around so we don't have to keep up this whole girlfriend/boyfriend appearance, but then he threads his fingers through mine, holding my hand as we walk toward the parking lot.

"I need to talk to you somewhere private. Figured my car is the best place to do it," he explains. "Plus, there's some papers in there I want you to look at."

"Okay." I'm so confused, not just about these papers he wants me to see but because he's holding my hand.

West and I are holding hands, and no one is around to see it. I should pull back, right? Part of me wants to, but the other part of me wants to continue holding his hand so my fingers won't long to wrap around the bottle of a spray can.

"There's some stuff I need to tell you, too," I inform him. "Once you're done telling me your stuff."

He glances at me with his brows furrowed. "Everything okay?"

I waver. "That's debatable. And honestly, I don't think we should discuss it while we're out in the open."

He frowns but nods, not saying anything else. We remain quiet for the rest of the walk to his car. When we reach it, he opens the passenger door for me and gestures for me to climb in.

"Still pretending we're a gentleman?" I joke as I move to get in.

"Still pretending like you don't like it?" he quips with a grin, but I detect the slightest bit of sadness in his eyes, a reminder of all the crap he's dealing with beneath the jokes and smiles.

I'm about to ask him if he's okay, but he shuts the door. Then he rounds the front of his car and climbs into the driver's seat.

"So, what happened this morning with your parents?" I ask after he shuts the door.

"That's what I want to talk to you about." He reaches into the back seat, picks up a folder, and sets it down on my lap.

I cock my head to the side. "What is this?"

"Some papers my parents tried to get me to sign," he explains with a trace of irritation in his voice. "They wouldn't tell me what they were for, so I took them and ran."

My eyes widen. "You ran?"

He lifts a shoulder, his jaw set tight as he gazes out the window. "If I didn't, my dad … well, he would've made me sign them."

West has said a few things here and there that made me wonder if his father was abusive. I haven't flat-out asked him yet, mostly because I'm not sure how to approach the subject without upsetting him.

"What do you mean by *make you*?" I ask, measuring his reaction.

He just shrugs and shakes his head. "It doesn't really matter."

"No, it does." Sucking in a quiet breath, I reach over and place my hand on his cheek.

When he jolts from the touch, I start to pull back. "Sorry."

But he quickly places a hand over mine and keeps my hand against his cheek again. "You don't ever have to be sorry for touching me."

My heart is thudding so loudly that the noise fills my head. "I just … I want to make sure you're okay. Some of the things you say … they make me wonder if … they make me wonder just how bad things are for you at home."

His throat muscles work as he swallows hard. "It doesn't really matter anymore. That home is no longer my home. I pretty much sealed that deal when I took off with these papers."

Thinking about what he told me the other day, about how his parents could destroy his life, worry stirs through me. Plus, he's living in that sketchy house, which is not a replacement home, in my opinion.

"What're you going to do then?" I ask. "I mean, where are you going to live?"

He gives a half-shrug. "I'm not sure yet, but if those papers are what I think they are, I may not have to worry about money anymore, which eliminates at least one of my problems."

My gaze drops to the folder that he tossed into my lap. "What are they?"

"Well, from what I can tell, someone died and left me a

bunch of money. And if I signed those papers, all that money would be transferred over to my parents."

My gaze darts up to him. "That's what they wanted to talk to you about this morning?"

"Yep," he says tightly. "And like I said, my dad was going to try to force me to sign them, but I ran."

I swallow hard. "Why would they do that? I mean, aren't your parents, like, loaded?"

"That's what I thought, and we've always lived that way, but my parents are also the kind of people that would fake their wealth. But I know my dad makes a lot of money." He wavers, chewing on his bottom lip. "My mom also likes to spend a lot of money, though."

"Maybe they got into financial trouble then," I suggest. "Although, that doesn't give them the right to try to steal your money."

"I know," he assures me. "I just wish I knew who left me the money."

"Do the papers give a name?"

"Yeah, they do." He reaches in front of me, causing my hand to fall from his cheek. Then he opens the folder. Inside is a stack of papers, which he sifts through until he finds the one he's looking for. "I think that's who it is right there." He taps a name printed on one of the pages.

"Charlotte Everlyson," I read the name aloud then glance at him. "Do you know who that is?"

He shakes his head, wisps of his blond hair falling

across his forehead. "No." He pauses, hesitancy written all over his face. "But I'm wondering if maybe it's my real mom."

My heart breaks for him in ways I didn't think were possible. "Did your mom …? Did Loraine confirm that you were adopted?"

"No," he utters quietly, looking away from me. "I didn't really have a chance to ask her about it. I was there for, like, two minutes before my dad started threatening me and getting in my face."

My heart breaks even more for him.

When my parents died, it nearly broke me because, in that moment, I lost love. West, though, he's never had that kind of love.

"West," I start carefully. "Has your dad …? Has he …?"

His gaze glides to mine. "Has he what?"

I swallow down the thickness building in my throat. "Has he ever hit you?"

When he doesn't answer right away, almost looking a bit ashamed, my heart literally splits open and bleeds out. Unsure what to do or say, I reach out and place my hand against his cheek again, because he seems to kind of like that.

"You need to tell someone. He can't just get away with stuff like that."

He shakes his head. "No one would believe me; trust

me. My parents have this entire town wrapped around their fingers."

I skim my finger along his cheekbone. "You have to do something. You can't just keep dealing with it silently."

"I'm not," he murmurs. "I moved out."

"Yeah, but …" I press my lips together, pausing to collect myself. "That place you're staying at probably shouldn't be a long-term solution."

He arches a brow. "You worried about me, Alexis Baker?"

I pretend to be really conflicted about it, but the straight-up truth is that I am.

"Maybe a little bit."

The corners of his lips twitch, like he's about to smile, but he never quite gets there. "Well, hopefully, these papers are what I think they are. Or, well, at least that someone left me a sum of money. Then I can afford to move out of that house and get my own place."

"How do you find out for sure?"

"Well, I'd say talk to a lawyer, but considering my dad knows every lawyer in town, I'll probably have to go to one in a different town."

"It might take a few days to make an appointment," I tell him. "So maybe you can make one and, until then, Loki could look at these papers and tell us what they are. He's an adult and deals with business-y stuff all the time. Plus, I think he took a couple of law classes in college."

"You'd ask him to do that?" he asks, surprised.

I shrug. "Sure. Why not?"

"I don't know …" He nibbles on his bottom lip, searching my eyes for something. What? I haven't got a clue. When he speaks again, he throws me for a total loop. "I want to kiss you."

My brows knit. *"Right now?"* I peer out the window at the parking lot. Not a single person in sight. "But there's no one around."

"I know." He brushes his fingers along my cheek, drawing my attention back to him. "I just want to kiss you, though."

His words remind me of what the blackmailer told me to do. How I'm supposed to play West. How he's in love with me.

I need to tell West about what happened, and now is the perfect moment to do so.

But then West is leaning forward and brushing his lips against mine and, for a mind-numbing instant, I forget about everything.

And then he deepens the kiss, tangling his tongue with mine, and all other thoughts go *peace out*. A soft groan leaves his lips as he kisses me again. And again. And again.

I know I should pull back. There's no one around, so this isn't part of the pretending. Plus, there's so much I need to tell him. But he keeps kissing me, combing his fingers through my hair and gently pulling at the roots. It feels so damn good that I can barely think straight. Maybe that's why I start to lean closer to him, my waist pushing against the console uncomfortably. I hardly feel the discomfort, though, my hands unconsciously drifting toward him, up his chest, along the outside of his shirt.

He shudders, biting down on my bottom lip. A whimper, not in pain, but because it feels so good releases from me.

"Fucking hell, Lex," he whispers, his lips brushing against mine, his hands on my waist, stiff like he's struggling with whether or not to hold on to me.

Normally, this would be the point where I'd start thinking about the past, but my mind is way too hazy from all the sensations fluttering through me.

He rests his forehead against mine, his heavy breathing dusting across my face. His fingers delve into my waist, his body quivering as he struggles with … something.

I'm not sure what to do. Pull back? Ask him if he's okay? Run? The old Alexis would've. Ran from the emotions coursing through me. But this new, weirdo Alexis, who apparently likes to kiss, the one who's trying to do better, stays where she is. Yet, she's conflicted.

"Are …? Are you okay?" My hands are resting on his chest where his heart is pounding.

He gives an unsteady nod. "Yeah, I am … I just …" He slightly leans back, opening his eyes. "I just …" Question marks fill his eyes.

It's like he's asking me a silent question and expecting me to answer. And, while I wish I was a mind reader in that moment, I'm not, so I have no idea what he wants me to say.

"Fuck," he breathes out then leans forward and kisses me again.

This kiss is much briefer, and then he's leaning back and looking at me, again questioningly.

Clearly, he wants something. And I'm not sure what.

"When I kissed you in the hallway to shut up Masie … you were okay with that, right?" he asks, holding my gaze.

I nod, confused. "Yeah … why?"

"I just … wanted to make sure." He reaches up and tucks a strand of my hair behind my ear. "And, are you okay with the kiss just barely?"

"Um … yeah …" I admit, but with a little bit less confidence than the last time.

While this question is similar, it's also different in a lot of ways. Because the kiss in front of Masie was for show. The kiss just barely was for … Well, I'm not positive what it was for. But I do know it definitely wasn't for our deal.

West is in love with you, the blackmailer told me.

What if he wasn't lying?

Before I can arrive at a conclusion, West is nodding. Then he dips his lips toward mine and kisses me again.

I start to notice how, the more I kiss him, the easier it

becomes. Not just because I'm getting used to kissing, but because I'm getting used to kissing West.

Because I'm starting to like kissing him.

Oh my God, I like kissing West!

I should pull back. I know I should. Instead, I kiss him back way more intensely than I ever have. He must like it, because he keeps groaning softly while clutching on to me, like he can somehow pull me closer than I already am. He can't, though, because the console is in the way.

Eventually, he decides to solve that problem and starts to pull me over it. It surprises me how eagerly I go to him, clambering over it and climbing onto his lap. Then nervousness creeps through me. And not just because I'm straddling his lap—well, that's part of it—but the other part is how much I can feel of him.

West is completely turned on.

As that thought registers in my brain, I tense.

He pulls back immediately, panting, out of breath. "You okay?" he asks, his lips slightly swollen.

I know if I say "no," he'll stop. West is a good guy and would never pressure me to do anything. That much I've decided about him. And if I say "yes," we'll keep kissing.

Resting my hands on his shoulders, I find myself nodding.

He hesitates, his hand finding my cheek. "If at any time you want to stop, just say so, okay?" He waits for me to nod then seals his lips to mine again, kissing me for … Well, I've lost count of how many times we've kissed. And that number keeps growing and growing the longer we stay in his car.

His tongue plays with mine as he kisses and bites and nips at my lips, causing me to moan in a way I don't even recognize.

"West," I murmur as I tip my head back, my mind spinning with dizziness.

"Mmm …" he hums, continuing to kiss me, making a path down to my jawline, my neck. Then he kisses me there, sweeping his tongue out and grazing across my skin, the metal of his tongue ring sending goosebumps sprouting across my skin. But that's nothing compared to when he grinds his hips against mine.

I gasp, squeezing my eyelids shut as I dig my fingernails into his shoulder blades.

He pauses, tension rolling off of him. "Lex?" A silent question floods his tone, asking, *do you want me to stop?*

Deep down, in the depths of my confused, broken, but maybe slightly healing soul, I know I should say yes. Know there's a ton of other stuff we should be doing, like talking about the blackmailer, what he told me. We also should be talking more about his parents. But this is the first time in a very long time when I've felt marginally content without paint staining my fingertips. So, I don't respond, simply rolling my hips against his.

"Shit," he mutters with his hands on my waist, that tension in his body amplifying.

Reality starts to trickle over me.

Maybe he doesn't want this.

Maybe he doesn't want me.

Maybe the blackmailer was lying.

You're so fucking ugly.

Nobody wants you.

You should just get rid of yourself.

I'm about to dive off his lap when he rolls his hips against mine while gently biting down on the side of my neck. This isn't the first time he's bitten me in this spot, although it was much gentler last time. And unlike last time, I remain where I am, holding on to him instead of pushing him away.

He does the movement again with his hips, over and over again. Then he moves his mouth from my neck, but only to make his way up to my lips where he kisses me so deeply that I forget how to breathe.

Just like I've basically forgotten where I am.

However, a reminder that we're making out heavily in his car in the school parking lot greets us moments later in the form of a knock on the window.

We jerk back, gasping for air, my pulse soaring so swiftly that I swear the damn idiot is about to give out on me.

I turn to see who knocked then a frown forms on my face.

"Shit," West mutters as he glances outside the window at the monitor who walks around during school hours and makes sure no one does … well, basically what West and I were just doing.

"Yeah, shit for sure," I agree, knowing we're about to get detention.

When West looks at me with a trace of a smile on his lips, I'm not sure that I'm that sad about that fact. At least, not sad about the fact that we kissed and touched. In fact, it might be worth the punishment we're about to get.

As I realize this, realize how much I liked kissing him, it freaks me the hell out for several different reasons. One being I haven't gotten to tell him about what the blackmailer wants me to do, which means, technically, everything I do with West could be used against us. And another one is that I'm realizing that I'm not sure I was ever in love with Blaine. Not that I'm in love with West. But I never, ever felt this way about Blaine—all reckless and out of control to the point where I can't think straight. It sort of scares me, knowing I may be over Blaine since it means letting go of something connected to my past. It might be time to do it, though. Let the past go and focus on the future.

A couple of weeks ago, I couldn't even think about the future, but maybe that's because I was grasping on to the past too much. Like with my feelings for Blaine and my friendship with Masie. And this thing that happened with Jay, I've never dealt with that, and I honestly didn't want to. But then West found out, and I felt a bit freer in that moment. Still sort of do.

That doesn't mean that acknowledging all of this is easy. No.

As I flick through all these thoughts in my mind, panic takes hold of me. I want to run. Boy, do I. But I don't. Instead, I get out of the car and face my punishment head-on, which is definitely a first for me.

4

WEST

I HAVE NEVER BEEN SO TURNED on in my life than while I was making out with Alexis in my car. The way she tastes, the way she kept shivering every time I grazed my teeth along the side of her neck, I felt like I was about to explode. But, in the back of my mind, part of me whispered to stop, that Lex and I need to talk about what Ellis discovered about her blackmailer.

Then she rolled her hips against mine, and I damn near lost it.

I wanted her so much.

I want her so much.

I want to kiss her all the time.

I want to taste her lips until it's all I can taste.

But it's not just kissing her that gets me going. No, it's the way that she talks to me and looks at me sometimes, like she cares. It's part of the reason I fell for her—that beneath her trying-to-be-all-badass, I-don't-give-a-shit-about-anything exterior, she has the sweetest heart. Not that she isn't badass. She's probably the most badass girl I've ever met. Strong as hell, too. I just hope that when I tell her what I found out about her blackmailer, she won't put that wall up around herself again.

God, I hate Blaine, I think to myself as I sit in afterschool detention. But the person I hate the most? Jay.

I briefly saw him in the hallway earlier today, laughing with his friends like he doesn't have a care in the world. It made rage simmer underneath my skin. After seeing that video, after finding out what he did to Lex, I want nothing more than to beat his fucking ass. And while Lex may have told me not to do anything, I fully plan on doing something. I just need a plan and a way not to get caught.

Lex is sitting in a desk toward the front of the classroom, due to the hall monitor's request that we shouldn't be allowed to sit together. We also have afterschool detention and lunch detention for the next week. While I'm not too worried about myself, considering I've basically cut ties with my parents, I am concerned Lex is going to get in a lot of trouble, especially since she just got busted for that whole spray painting thing. Not to mention the fact that somehow people have found out about our little make-out session in the car and rumors are floating around. Not that I give a shit. But Lex might. Though, she didn't seem that freaked out when I kissed her in front of Masie, an impulsive decision I made when I saw Masie basically telling the entire school that Lex was in love with Blaine. And I know the bitch did it on purpose to humiliate Lex. She might not be able to see it, and I'm not about to tell her, but Masie is the kind of person who makes herself feel better by putting down the people around her. She's been doing that shit to Lex for years now.

Anyway, I haven't gotten a chance to talk to Lex since we were caught making out. The hall monitor made a point to escort us to class, and then we had lunch detention that lasted until the bell rang and she basically ran out of the classroom. I texted her during fifth period, but she never replied. And I didn't see her again until she walked into afterschool detention. She didn't even meet my gaze when she hurried in. I'll admit that has me worried.

Sneaking a glance up at the teacher monitoring detention, I dig out my phone and send her a text, ignoring all the messages I've receive from Loraine and Eli. While I know I'll probably have to read them eventually, I don't want to deal with them just yet.

No, what I want to focus on right now is Lex.

Me: You doing okay up there?

She jolts a little as the message buzzes through. Then, holding her phone underneath the desk, she discreetly reads the message. She doesn't answer right away, and my worry grows that maybe she isn't going to. Then my phone vibrates in my hand.

Lex: Yeah. What about you?

I chew on my lip, deliberating how I want to reply. Should I be careful and just keep my answer simple? Or should I be open and flirty with her? Be who I am. Normally, I'd be cautious with her, not wanting to scare her off. But, after what happened in the car between us ...

Me: I'm doing fucking great, actually. It's amazing how detention isn't as bad when you've got all these sexy as hell memories to play on repeat in your head.

I hit *send* and wait for her response. It takes her about a minute to do so, but it's worth it.

Lex: Yeah, well, I've got more than just the memories to remind me. There are reminders all over my neck.

A smile curves at my lips.

Me: I gave you hickeys, huh?

I glance up at her and find her sweeping her hair across her shoulder, probably in an attempt to hide the hickeys.

Lex: Yeah. I tried to cover them up before I came here, but it's a lost cause. Probably doesn't really matter anyway, since everyone found out about what happened. Though I have no idea how.

Me: I didn't tell anyone, I swear.

Lex: I didn't think it was you.

The fact that she didn't automatically accuse me makes my heart do weird things.

Me: I'm pretty sure someone saw us. Well, other than Cranky Pants Mcgee, the good old creepy hall monitor.

Lex: What's really creepy is that who knows how long she stood there watching us before tapping on the window.

I smash my lips together, holding back a laugh.

Me: Wow, you've got quite the little perverted mind, Alexis Baker.

Lex: Probably because I've been hanging out with you so much lately.

Me: Hanging out? Is that what you wanna call our constant, hot make-out sessions?

When she doesn't answer right away, I wonder if perhaps I pushed her too far. Then she replies, and a smile curves across my lips.

Lex: It's not my fault you keep kissing me all the time. My lips must be really irresistible.

I sink my teeth into my bottom lip as images of kissing those irresistible lips of hers replay through my mind.

Me: Oh, they fucking are.

Lex: I was just kidding.

Me: And I was definitely not kidding. Your lips are the most irresistible thing I've ever tasted. Like ever.

Lex: You're such a freak.

Me: And you're the most beautiful girl I've ever seen.

I wait for her to respond, but a message doesn't pop up right away. I can see the dots on the screen, though, so I know she read the message. Eventually, she texts me again, and honestly, I don't know what to make of it.

Lex: We need to talk after detention is over. Meet me out in the hallway?

Like I was just going to take off.

Still, the way her message seemed to shift to formal has me concerned.

What if she wants us to just be friends?

What if she tries to put an end to …?

I shake my head at myself. Put an end to what? None of this was ever supposed to be real to her. We were supposed to be fake dating, though I had hoped it'd lead to more. But that doesn't mean she wants it to. Honestly, I'm not sure what she wants. For all I know, she could just pity me.

Great, this awesome plan of mine is turning into a real disaster.

Just like my life.

But I am going to do one thing right.

Taking out my phone, I send a text I've been meaning to send all day before Loraine and Eli distracted me.

Me: We need to talk.

Blaine: I've got nothing to say to you, asshole.

Me: You may not have anything to say right now, but you might after I tell you why we need to talk.

Blaine: Go fuck yourself. The moment you sucker-punched me, you lost your privilege to talk to me.

I roll my eyes. *Privilege.* Like it's some sort of honor to talk to him.

Me: How about this then? We're gonna talk about why Lex has been getting texts from an unknown number that's registered in your name.

When he doesn't answer right away, I know. Know that he's somehow involved with this. Deep down, I think I'd been hoping Ellis was somehow wrong. Not because I want to stay friends with Blaine—our friendship ended the moment he broke Lex's heart. No, I'm worried how Lex is going to handle this. Worry that her heart is going to get broken all over again.

Blaise: Meet me at my house at six.

That's all he says, but it's enough for me to be certain.

Certain that he's part of this.

5

ALEXIS

I'M a nervous wreck during the rest of detention, for a few reasons, one being that I know Loki is going to be super upset with me when I get home. And two being that, after detention, I'm going to force myself to talk to West about what the blackmailer told me. Because, if I don't, then I'm basically playing their game. And while I may have never said I wasn't going to play their game, I know I can't. At least, not for reals. If I talk to West, maybe we can come up with our own plan to play with the blackmailer.

I also need to talk to him about our fake relationship, because the line between what's real and just pretend is starting to get blurry.

As detention comes to an end, I make my way out of the classroom then linger in the hallway, waiting for West to come out.

While I'm standing there, going over what I should say to him, my phone goes off. I immediately tense, wondering if it's the blackmailer. Nope. It's Loki

Loki: Don't forget that you're supposed to go straight to the store to paint it after you get out of detention. And then, when you get home, we're going to sit down and have a little talk about what happened today.

Which means he's going to chew my butt out for getting detention. Or maybe he's just going to tell me it's time to move out, that he is officially done with me. He kind of made it clear the day I got hauled to the police station that he was tired of my crap. Maybe this was the final straw. I am going to be turning eighteen soon, so he could tell me to move out.

I don't know, though. Loki isn't that hardcore, no matter how much he pretends to be.

Me: I figured as much. And I'm heading to the store in just a few. I didn't forget.

Sighing quietly at that thought, I put my phone away and wait for West, who's gotten trapped in a conversation with the teacher monitoring the classroom today, who also happens to be the PE teacher and coach. West used to play a lot of sports before he just up and quit, so he knows the coach pretty well.

The hallways are fairly vacant as I wait, something I'm relieved about since everyone has been gawking and whispering about me all day. Some were discussing the fight that went down between Masie and me, while others were gossiping about my and West's heavy make-out session in the car. It's annoying. Not that I care that anyone saw us making out. I mean, that was sort of the point of us fake dating in the first place. However, I'm not a fan of gossip. Masie used to do it all the time, and it was annoying.

"Hey," West says as he exits the classroom with a few books in his hand. He offers me a small, somewhat nervous smile as he stops in front of me. "Sorry I got us detention. I know you were already in trouble. I hope this doesn't make it worse."

I give a dismissive wave of my hand. "It's not your fault. I chose to be part of … what happened in the car."

What did even happen in the car? Was that all pretend? Or did West really want to kiss me?

Do I really want to kiss West?

I sort of do, and that scares the crap out of me.

Hesitancy is written all over his face as he assesses me. "You're okay with what happened?"

"You mean with getting detention?" I shrug. "I've gotten detention before."

He slowly shakes his head, his gaze welded to mine. "No, with what happened in the car between us."

"Oh." My fingers unconsciously drift to where a hickey is branding my skin, memories of how it got there floating dizzily through my mind. Then I sink my teeth into my bottom lip. "I'm fine with that … I just …" I grimace. "I just don't get exactly what happened between us."

A crooked, amused smile touches his lips as he brushes the pad of his thumb along my bottom lip. "Well, first we kissed, and then I bit your neck." His gaze briefly strays to the spot marking the moment. Then he leans in and lowers his voice. "And then you grinded against me over and over again." He kisses me then, just a light brush of lips. And once again, all thoughts vacate my mind as I reach up and hold his shoulders as I kiss him back.

Yesterday, when I drew a sketch of him, I wanted to erase the pain that haunted his eyes. Apparently, my dumb ass thought that meant kissing him. A lot. So much so that I forget about everything else. Like the fact that I'm supposed to be at a store, painting over my art.

Thankfully, my phone goes off inside my pocket and yanks me away from lust land.

I move back, breaking the kiss, my breathing coming out in heavy pants as I dig my phone out.

I honestly thought it'd be Loki again, but nope. It's from the blackmailer. And his words, they bitch smack me back into reality.

Unknown: Look at you, doing such a damn good job at playing this game. Although, if I didn't know any better, I'd think you were enjoying yourself. But we both know that you're in love with Blaine.

"What's wrong?" A crease forms between West's brows

as his gaze bounces back and forth between my face and my phone.

"Um ..." I swallow hard, highly aware that the blackmailer is more than likely watching me from somewhere, but I have no clue where since no one appears to be around. That doesn't mean someone isn't spying on us from one of the many classrooms nearby. After everything they've done to me, I'm not surprised. It still makes me anxious, though.

"It's nothing. I just need to get going." I stuff my phone into my pocket and move to leave, but he captures my arm and pulls me back to him.

"Baby, just talk to me," he pleads.

Normally, I'd chew out his ass for calling me baby, but now really isn't the time to worry about that.

I subtly shake my head then mutter under my breath, "Not now. Can you meet me at my house later?" Then, more loudly, I ask, "You know, so we can work on that project for Biology."

Tension pours off him as he nods. "Yeah, I'll stop by around seven?"

I nod, giving him a grateful look, glad he caught on. He doesn't let me go, though. Instead, he threads his fingers through mine.

When I give him a puzzled look, he explains, "I'll walk you to your car."

"Oh. Okay." I clutch his hand, my gaze sweeping the

hallway as we walk down it and push out the doors, stepping into the warm, spring air.

Despite the warmth, I feel chilly inside. Unsettled. Nervous. It makes me realize how distracted I was with West today. Makes me want to go back to that moment in the car with him. Unfortunately, I still don't know where we stand, especially when I climb into my car and he lowers his head to kiss me goodbye.

"I'll see you at seven," he whispers, his lips hovering close to mine. "Drive safe. And if you need anything at all, call me."

I bob my head up and down, my heart a mess inside my chest. "Okay."

He steps back, and I shut the door then drive out of the parking lot.

As I'm nearing the exit, I glance in the rearview mirror and find him watching me drive away, his eyes crammed with worry. I can't decide if that's any better than the sadness that I saw haunt them yesterday.

6

WEST

WHEN I ARRIVE at Blaine's house, I'm completely on edge, feeling like I'm about to crawl out of my skin with restlessness, with irritation, with a lot of things.

As I'm climbing out of the car, I receive a text that amplifies that uneasiness.

Holden: We have a job to do tonight. Be at the house by ten.

My jaw ticks as I type a reply.

Me: I can't go out that late. It's a school night.

Holden: I don't really give a shit what night it is. You're gonna go or else.

That's all he says. He doesn't even bother with giving a list of what will happen if I don't show. But he doesn't have to. He already made it pretty damn clear what'll happen if I back out of working for him.

"You don't just get to quit this, man," he had told me when I tried to quit. *"I brought you into this; vouched for you. And you don't get to quit until I say you do. And if you try, there will be consequences. Not just from me, but from my boss. When you agreed to my job offer, you agreed to stay in this until we let you go. Well, unless you don't mind being thrown into the lake with bricks tied to your feet."*

While I'm not positive if he was just trying to scare me or was telling the truth, it was enough to terrify me into continuing this shitshow of dealing at night. That doesn't mean I'm not plotting my way out of this mess. I just need to get ahold of this money, and then I can take off and start a new life, away from Honeyton, away from drug dealing, and away from the people I thought were my parents. Although, that means being away from Lex.

For a brief moment, my thoughts wander to the idea of what it'd be like if she came with me, but then I pull my head out of dreamland and focus on reality. And the reality is that, until I have the money, I'm stuck here.

So, I text Holden back.

Me: Okay.

Then I hop out of the car, tuck my phone into my back pocket, and start toward Blaine's house. His father's patrol car isn't parked in the driveway, something I'm grateful for, since the last time I saw him was right after I punched Blaine and he drove me home instead of arresting me.

About halfway up the pathway, the front door swings

open and out walks someone with a hoodie pulled over their head. I slow down, unsure what the hell is going on, when I hear the person mutter, "Get in your car."

Blaine. But, why the hell is he dressed like someone who's about to rob a place?

"Dude, what're you doing?" I ask as he strides toward me.

"Just get in the car," he mutters as he nears me. "Now, for fuck's sake."

Awesome. He's already pissing me off.

"Whatever," I mutter then turn around and get back in my car.

He stops beside the passenger side of the door, peers around, then ducks in. Once he's in the seat, he hunkers down. "Start driving," he instructs.

I roll my eyes but start up the car. "Where do you want me to go?"

"Go up by the lake," he mumbles as he tugs the hood of his jacket farther down his face.

"Why?" I question, eyeing him over. "And what the hell's your deal? Why're you dressed like that?"

He sneaks a peek out the window. "Because I might be being watched. And I'm not supposed to be talking to you. Well, not in private. So, drive up to the lake. Go to that spot where you, Lex, Masie, and I would go sometimes. You know, the one we found that one time where no one ever goes."

I'd think he lost his damn mind, except I can't help thinking of all the weird stuff going on with Lex.

"What if whoever's following you follows us up there?" I point out, reaching for my shifter.

"Make sure no one does," he says, glancing at me. "Drive like that time we egged Mr. M.'s house and he nearly caught us."

"Okay," I say, backing down the driveway. "But if I get pulled over, your dumbass is paying for the ticket."

BLAINE and I hardly speak while we make the drive up to the lake. Not that I don't try. Every time I attempt to get a conversation going, he shuts it down while giving paranoid glances over his shoulder at the road behind us like he's looking for a car tailing us. I don't see anyone behind us and, truthfully, by the time we arrive at our spot, I wonder if he's on something.

"I think we're good," he mutters as he straightens in the seat and looks around at the trees surrounding us.

The dirt road we took up here is bumpy and dead ends where I parked so no one can come up here without us knowing.

"Dude, what's your problem?" I ask as I turn off the engine, watching him continue to look around the forest like he's expecting a monster to jump out of the trees or something. "Are you on something?"

"No. Although, I wish I was." He bounces his knee up and down as he pulls out his phone. "Good. We have no signal up here." He pockets his phone and lets out a relieved exhale, his head falling back against the headrest as he closes his eyes. "I am so fucked, man."

"Good for you," I say in a cold tone. "But that's not why I brought you up here." I rotate in the seat to face him. "Why in the hell are you blackmailing Lex?"

Shaking his head from side to side, he opens his eyes and looks at me. "I'm not."

"Then why is the unknown number that's been sending her texts registered in your name?"

He swallows hard, his haze straying to the window. "Because that's what they wanted me to do."

"Who the hell are *they*?" I press.

He shakes his head and shrugs. "I have no idea."

I open and flex my hands, struggling to stay calm. "Look, I'm trying not to get pissed until I have some answers, but this vague answer shit is really starting to piss me off."

"I'm not trying to be vague on purpose." When he looks at me again, I see something that makes me pause. Fear. He's fucking afraid of something. "I really don't know who's doing it. All I know is that whoever is blackmailing Lex is also blackmailing me, and one of the things they did was have me open up that unknown phone line. I didn't send any of the texts, and I hate myself for being part of this, but what these people have on me ..." He balls his hands into fists and lets out a shaky exhale. "If anyone finds out what they know about me, I'll go to jail."

It takes me a moment to process everything he just said. And even then, I'm still not sure I'm following him.

"So, what you're saying is there's some sort of group that blackmailed you into opening a phone line that they could use to blackmail Alexis?" Saying it aloud sounds weird as fuck. "But you have no idea who this group is?"

He gives a nod, glancing at me again. "A few months ago, I received this text from an unknown number. Attached to it was a video of me ... Anyway, there was some stuff on that video that no one can find out I did. So I did what they asked me to do."

"And all they wanted you to do was open a phone line for them?"

"No. They've had me do a lot of stuff; one being hook up with Masie."

My gut twists at that. He's not really dating Masie? If this is true, then I have to tell Lex. And then what? Will she go back to liking him? I'm not sure.

"Is Masie part of this?"

"No. She has no idea."

"So you're playing her?"

"You say that like you care," he bites out. "You don't

even like her."

"I know. I'm just wondering why this person blackmailing you had you hook up with her."

He lifts a shoulder with his jaw set tight. "I honestly have no idea what they're trying to do. All I know is that I'm going to do what they ask because there's no way I'm letting that video get out."

"Why?" I ask curiously. "What's on it?"

He glares at me. "Like I'd tell you. I know where we stand. The only reason I met up with you is because you found out about the number. Speaking of which, how did you figure out I opened the account?"

"You have your secrets, and I have mine," I reply vaguely. "Maybe if you share yours, I'll share mine."

He quickly shakes his head. "I'm not telling you what's on the video."

My mind fills up with all sorts of ideas of what he could've possibly done, ranging from cheating in school to robbing a store. I used to feel like I knew him, but now I feel like he's a stranger. Still, that doesn't mean we can't work together to figure out who this fucker blackmailing everyone is.

"I'm going to figure out who's behind this," I inform him. "You want to help?"

He wavers. "I don't know … If they find out I'm helping you, they could release that video."

"Then don't let them find out. All you need to do is text

me if you find out any information that could help figure out who they are."

He promptly shakes his head. "I can't text about this. They sometimes hack into my phone, which is part of the reason why I had you drive us up here. No signal means they can't track my phone or open my Facetime app without me knowing."

"So they're good with tech stuff," I state. "That's a good starting point."

He folds his arms across his chest, looking vulnerable and weak. "Look, I want to figure out who they are, too, but I'm not going to, like, try to find them. But if I discover anything that could be helpful, I'll let you know in a non-electronic way." He pauses, glancing at me. "Why are you doing this, anyway? Are they blackmailing you, too?"

I shake my head, brushing a couple strands of hair out of my eyes. "No."

He studies me for a second. "Then why are you doing it?"

I shrug. "To help Lex."

A small smile touches his lips. "I knew it."

I glare at him. "Knew what?"

"Knew that you fucking liked her. I've wondered for a while, but when you sucker-punched me, I figured I was right."

"Yeah, man, I do," I admit.

What I don't say, though, is that it probably doesn't

matter anymore. That once I tell Lex what I found out, she may forgive Blaine. That she may go back to loving him, and then I'll be left with a broken heart. Not that it'll be Lex's fault. She thinks our relationship and my feelings for her aren't real, because that's what I told her. Because I was too afraid to tell the truth.

Always covering up my feelings.

Story of my life.

I'm really starting to get tired of it.

"We should probably get going," Blaine tells me after a minute ticks by and no one says anything.

I check the time on the clock on the dashboard and nod. "Yeah, you're probably right."

We grow quiet as I start up the car and begin the drive back to his house.

Blaine receives a text the moment we get a signal again, and whatever the message contains seems to cause anxiety to burst through him.

"What's up?" I ask after about the fifteenth time of him fidgeting with the hood of his jacket.

"It's nothing," he mumbles, scratching his wrist.

"You're lying. We might not really be friends anymore, but we used to be, so I can tell when you're nervous."

"I said I'm fine," he bites out, crossing his arms.

"Whatever," I give in, deciding I'm tired of his shit.

Silence stretches between us for another minute or two, and then he heaves out a loud exhale.

"I just received a text from them," he suddenly grumbles. "They know you're with me, and they … they want me to pick a fight with you."

My brows knit. "Why?"

He gives a stiff half-shrug. "I already told you that I have no idea why they do the things they do. But what I do know is that, if I don't beat your ass up by the time we get to my house, I'm screwed. And I don't want to, I really don't, but I also can't … No one can see that video."

Again, I want to know what's on the video they have of him.

I thrum my fingers on top of the shifter as I make the last turn into the neighborhood where his house is located, trying to figure out what to do. If he tries to beat me up, I'm going to fight back, and that'll probably lead to both of us getting arrested, though I'll be the one ending up in more trouble. But I'm not just going to stand there and let him kick my ass either.

"Okay, here's what we're going to do," I tell him as I slow down at the edge of his driveway. "We're gonna get out of the car. I'll let you get a few swings in, and I'll take one at you. Then you'll hit me one final time, and I'll pretend to fall to the ground hard. Hopefully, that'll satisfy them."

"Okay." He gives an uneven nod. "That might work."

"Just don't hit me in, like, the ribs or places where I'll break bones."

"All right." He's busting with nerves as I park the car at the end of the driveway. "Why're you doing this? We're not really friends anymore."

I shrug as I shift the car into park. "We were once." Besides, I can handle a little pain. I've had to for my entire life.

"Just remember that you owe me now," I add. "So if you find out anything about these blackmailers, you have to tell me."

He nods, and then we both get out of the car to kick each other's ass. Again.

I just hope it'll be worth it. That getting punched around a bit will help us get to whoever the hell is blackmailing both him and Lex.

7

ALEXIS

THE STORE OWNER isn't a big douchebag like I expected him to be. He's in his late-fifties probably, but looks more like a hippy old dude than just an uptight old dude. Honestly, he kind of reminds me of my dad with how laidback he's being about all this.

"As beautiful as the poem was," he tells me as he hands me a bucket of paint, a paintbrush, and a drop to put under me so I don't get paint all over the concrete, "it just can't be on the side of my store. You should consider writing a book of poetry. My niece does that sort of stuff and sells them online."

"Um … yeah, maybe I'll look into it," I tell him but don't really have any plans of doing so. Not right now anyway.

No, right now, I have way too much other stuff going

on to worry about things like that. Although, maybe when this is all over, I should sit down and start figuring out future stuff. After all, I'm going to be graduating soon. I'm going to need some sort of plan other than hanging around in Honeyton and making bad choices that lead to me getting stuck painting the sides of buildings and getting blackmailed by some asshole.

Blowing out a breath, I leave the inside of the store and go out into the alleyway to paint over the words I stained on the wall. When I did it, I had just found out about Masie and Blaine. It was just a few days ago, but so much has happened since then that it feels like a different time. I got hauled to the police station, Loki basically begged me to clean up my act, Zhara started talking to me again, West and I kissed—a lot—and he found out what happened between Jay and me. I almost feel like my soul was split open and is now trying to heal.

What changed, though? Sure, all of that stuff happened, but the catalyst, the moment everything shifted in my life, seems to lead back to that day I found Masie and Blaine making out in that pool. Why? Was it just because the last piece of my past shattered?

Who the crap knows? Truthfully, I probably should be worry about other stuff, like getting answers to the questions on my list in my notebook. What I wouldn't give to be like a PI or something. Then I'd know what to do.

Unfortunately, I'm just Alexis Baker, troublemaker extraordinaire.

Sighing at that thought, I get busy with painting the side of the building. Luckily, the paint color is an exact match, so I shouldn't have to go over the entire wall. I think it's still going to need a couple of coats since the color I used is dark blue, nearly black, and the wall is a light cream.

As I lift the paintbrush up and down, I read over the words I wrote:

Today, she learned the definition of betrayal.
A thorn got lodged in her heart,
But her heart was already woven with thorns,
So really, did the betrayal matter?
Maybe one day she'll find out.
But maybe she won't.
Not everything has an answer.
— Signed with a Kiss

I pause then lower the paintbrush, set it down, and take out my phone to take a quick picture of the poem. While I in no way, shape, or form want to relive what I was feeling in that moment, I do want the reminder of where I went and how I got out of there. And, even though the words are sort of haunting, they're my words. They belong to me. They are part of me, like the scars on my body. These scars, though, are pink and not quite healed, but are working on it.

Once I get my photo, I put my phone away then spend the next fifteen minutes covering up my poem. Then I balance the paintbrush on top of the bucket and decide to head into the store to buy a drink while I wait for it to dry so I can add a second coat.

Mid-turn, a loud bang echoes through the alleyway. I stiffen, my gaze sweeping across the trashcans and crates covering the narrow area. While nighttime hasn't settled yet, the sun has started to set and has taken some of the light with it, so everything is shadowed.

Uneasiness stirs inside me.

Maybe it's just a cat?

Convincing myself to chill the heck out, I hurry toward the door. I'm a handful of steps away when a figure appears at the end of the alleyway. They're wearing a hoodie pulled over their head and are dressed in all black with a pair of gloves covering their hands. Warning flags immediately start popping up everywhere.

My gaze strays to the door. It's about halfway between us. If I run for it, are they going to run? Will I make it before they do? And who are they? Do I even need to be worried? Or is this whole blackmailer thing just making me extremely paranoid?

I'm not sure.

What I do know is that running for the door is definitely the best option, because I'm not about to stick around and find out if this is part of the blackmailer's game.

So, I take off in a mad sprint toward the door.

So do they.

And in that moment, I feel a sort of fear I've never experienced before.

Pure and undiluted terror.

Even worse, the person is fast. Faster than me. And halfway to the door, I become painfully aware that I'm not going to make it. So, in a desperate, possibly brilliant or possibly stupid move, I spin around and run back the other way. Then I dig out my phone and start to dial the police, yelling over my shoulder, "I'm calling the police. And I'm taping this shit." The last part is a lie, but I don't know what else to do as I reach the end of the alleyway, which is a brick wall. It's about eight feet high, and a stack of crates are in front of it. I'm not sure if I can climb over in time, but I have to try, especially because I apparently have no signal back here.

Shit. Shit. Shit.

I pocket my phone, not slowing down, and leap onto the crates. I can hear heavy footsteps pounding after me as I jump up and launch myself toward the top of the wall. I manage to grab onto it and start to hoist myself over it when I feel fingers wrap around my ankle.

Panic seizes ahold of me as the person starts to drag me

back down, and I use my other foot to kick at them. I can't see what I'm doing, but I feel the heel of my thick boot smack against something, their face, I'm assuming by the way they cry out in pain. It does the trick, too, and they release their hold on me.

I move quickly, not glancing back as I haul my ass onto the wall. Then I jump down the other side, wincing as I twist my ankle. But I don't let it affect me. I run toward the front doors of the store. But right before I run inside, I glance over my shoulder at the wall.

No one is there.

that still doesn't bring me any sense of comfort. For all I know, they could be running around to the front of the store after me.

I go inside and duck down the nearest aisle. Then I lean against the shelf and struggle to catch my breath.

Crap. Crap. Crap. What the heck just happened? Better yet, what was that person planning on doing if they caught me? Was it just to scare me? Or was there a more sinister reason behind it? And does the blackmailer have anything to do with it?

I retrieve my phone from my pocket and check to see if I have any messages from them. Nope.

What's going on? Why is this happening? What do they want from me?

Pressure builds inside my chest, and I feel like screaming it out of me. But I know I can't do that right now, so I press my lips together and swallow it all down. Then I make my way over to the soda selection and pretend like I'm in here to buy a drink, which I was planning on doing anyway. But now I've got to figure out what to do.

If I tell someone what happened, will the blackmailer come after me? It's hard to decide the answer since I'm not sure if they're a part of it. If I don't tell anyone, though, I'll have to go back into that alleyway by myself and finish painting the wall.

I briefly close my eyes as anxiety lashes through me.

I don't know what to do.

I need help.

Taking a deep inhale, I call West.

"Hey," he answers after three rings. "What's up? No, let me guess. You couldn't wait until seven to hear my sexy voice."

A hollow sort of laugh slides past my lips.

West must sense something in the noise because he says, "What happened?"

"I don't ..." I peer around at all the customers nearby. For all I know, any of them could be the hooded person who chased me. "I need a favor. I'm at the store right now, and I was painting over my graffiti when ... this person showed up and sort of chased me. They didn't really do anything other than kind of scare me, and I'm not sure why they did it, but it has me nervous and worried, and I still need to go out and put another coat of paint on the wall, but I don't want to go out by myself. And I don't know who else to call, because I'm not sure if this has to do with the blackmailer or not. And I ..." I trail off, realizing that I'm rambling and that West hasn't said much of anything, which I find kind of strange. "Anyway, can you ...? Can you come here and hang out with me while I finish up? I mean, I get if you're, like, busy or something, but ..." I internally sigh. God, I sound pathetic. I hate asking for help. I'm desperate, though. And freaked out.

It takes West a few seconds to respond, and the growl in his tone startles me a bit. "Where are you right now?"

I chew on my thumbnail. "In the store."

"Okay, just stay there until I get there," he says intensely. "Don't go anywhere, okay?"

"O-okay," I stammer like a fucking idiot, but the fierceness in his tone was alarming. West is rarely intense, and almost always sarcastic, so this is definitely a side of him I haven't seen.

After we hang up, I spend the next five minutes pretending to be deeply engulfed in a dilemma of what soda I want when I'm really sneaking peeks at everyone and trying to figure out if they're the person who was in the alleyway, all while waiting for West to show up. I didn't think to ask him how long it'd take for him to get here. I probably should've because, eventually, I'm going to have to go outside before the owner notices that I'm not doing what I'm supposed to.

About seven minutes into my waiting, a person snags my attention. A guy, actually, maybe a few years older than me, with dark hair, dark eyes, and this weird circular tattoo on the side of his neck. He isn't wearing a hoodie or gloves, but he could've ditched those items easily. Not that any of this is suspicious, but the way he's watching me is.

He's standing on the other side of the shelf that I've been loitering in front of and keeps sneaking glances in my direction, only to look away when I glance at him. Finally, I can't take it anymore. Yeah, I may be scared and uneasy, but I'm not—and refuse to be—the kind of person who lets someone openly toy with me.

I turn toward him, crossing my arms. "Can I help you?"

A slow smile curves across his lips. "Yeah, actually." He steps toward me, and my heart instantly spikes. "You got a boyfriend, pretty girl?"

Oh my God, is he actually shitting me right now?

"Seriously?" I question. "That's your best pickup line?"

His smile grows. "I guess I'm a little off my *game* today."

The way he annunciates *game* makes me pause.

"I'll try to do better, though," he continues, his smile growing. "That is, if you don't have a boyfriend."

I think about what the blackmailer is having me do—pretend to date West so I can break his heart. They mentioned that I was going to play their game several times.

Is this the person who's been harassing me? If it is, then I'm even more confused since I have no clue who they are. Still, even the possibility that they could be sends a jolt of panic through me, and I start to back away from him.

"I have to go," I mutter then spin around to leave.

"What'd I say?" he asks innocently.

Then laughter hits my back as I duck down the closest aisle. I powerwalk about halfway down it then spin around to see if he's following me. No one's around, but I'm beyond nervous—

Arms suddenly encircle my waist. Then a slamming heartbeat of a second later, my back is touching someone's chest. I'm about one step away from going all self-defense and kicking some ass when a familiar voice whispers in my ear.

"Relax, baby," West says softly while stroking his fingers along my waist. "It's just me."

I exhale shakily then lean into him, seeking comfort in him for a moment. As the scent of his cologne and his warmth wraps around me, I find myself wanting to turn around, bury my head into his chest, and pretend the last half hour didn't happen.

"You okay?" he asks, kissing the back of my head.

I start to nod, but then I end up shaking my head, too freaked out to lie. "There was this guy, and he was talking to me, and he kept using words that the blackmailer uses. But I don't know if I was being paranoid, and I …" Heaving out a sigh, I spin around and face him. Then I instantly frown. "What the hell happened to your face?" I reach up to touch the cut running along his hairline, but then I pull back, worried touching it will hurt him.

He captures my fingers and draws my hand back up to him, placing my palm against his cheek. "Yeah, you might not be the only one who ran into a little bit of trouble."

I gape at him. "You were attacked?"

He tilts his head to the side, nuzzling against my palm. "No. Not necessarily attacked, but something sketchy happened. Unfortunately, the cut, I kind of did to myself by being a clumsy dumbass."

"What happened exactly?" I ask, picking up on him being vague.

He goes rigid, his gaze scanning the aisle behind me. "I'll tell you later when we're at your house. Right now, let's go get your beautiful, rebellious artwork cleaned up so we can go." He smiles at me, but tension is rippling off him.

Something is wrong. I can tell. So, I just nod.

He offers me a relieved look then threads his fingers through mine and lets me steer him toward where we need to go.

As I'm weaving down aisles and heading toward the back door, I keep throwing nervous glances around at every person we pass.

"You're nervous," West whisper softly. "Are you afraid the person who chased you came inside the store?"

Biting down on my bottom lip, I give a slight nod. "I'm not sure if they did, but that guy … he was acting really weird and seemed to be getting off on how twitchy he was making me. I took off down the aisle where you found me and haven't seen him since."

West skims his thumb along the back of my hand. "Dark hair? Dark eyes?"

I shrug. "He looked like every other dude out there, really. Well, except he had this circular mark on the side of his neck."

West wets his lips with his tongue, his thinking face on, as we reach the door that will take us outside into the alleyway.

I open it and step outside underneath the now dark sky, starlight and moonlight trickling into the alleyway and mixing with the light beside the door.

"Do you remember exactly what the mark looked like?" West asks, shutting the door behind us.

I nod. "Yeah. It was kind of weird looking … Honestly, it'd be better if I just drew it." I let go of his hand and avoid his gaze, busying myself with picking up the paintbrush. But I can feel his eyes on me, studying me, and I'm pretty sure I know what he's thinking.

You'll draw again?

Like Blaine and Masie, West also has noticed that I haven't drawn anything since my parents died.

"This paintbrush is kind of crusty," I say in an attempt to distract West from trying to dissect me with his beautiful, blue-eyed gaze. "I think I left it on top of the bucket for too long."

"Here. Let me see it." He takes the brush from me, makes his way over to a hose, rinses it off, and then shakes out the water. Then he returns back to me and with his gaze fixed on me, handing me back the brush.

I trap a shuddering breath inside my chest as his fingers brush against mine.

What the hell is wrong with me? Why am I acting so nervous suddenly?

I tell myself to knock it off, that if I should be nervous about anything, it should be over being chased earlier. But, as I start putting the last coat of paint on the wall, all I can concentrate on is him watching me.

Finally, I can't take it anymore.

"Why do you keep looking at me?" I demand.

He lifts a shoulder, propping his other shoulder against the wall as he continues to watch me. "I was just wondering when you started drawing again?"

I press my lips together as I move the paintbrush up and down. "It was actually yesterday."

"Really?" he asks, and I nod. He gives a short pause. "You okay with that?"

"Sure. Why wouldn't I be?"

"I just remember you saying how you've been struggling for quite a while with doing any sort of artwork. Well, besides graffiti." He says the last part jokingly and with a smile.

I roll my eyes, being playful for a bit. Then I sigh. "So I started drawing again. It's not that big of a deal." What I don't bother to mention, and never plan on mentioning, is that the first time I drew anything in almost a year, I ended up doing a sketch of him.

"Okay. Good." He decides to let me off the hook. "So, when we get back to your place tonight, you'll be okay with drawing the tattoo you saw on that guy's neck?"

I nod. "Yeah, I'll do my best. Although, I'm not really sure what having a drawing of it will help with."

"We can do an image search for it on the internet. That is, if you do a fantastic job at drawing it, which I know you will." Smiling, he tugs on a strand of my hair, causing my heart to flutter.

"I'll try to do a fantastic job," I inform him. "But I'm out of practice, so I might suck a bit."

"Lex, I've seen your art," he tells me in all seriousness. "Even on your worst day, your ability to create something beautiful with just a pencil and paper is amazing."

I'm getting really uncomfortable with his compliments, and I think he might sense it, since he changes the subject.

"I'm going to go look around here while you finish that up," he tells me as he backs away.

"Wait—you're not leaving the alleyway, right?" I ask in a panic.

He promptly shakes his head. "No, baby, I'm not leaving you," he promises. "I'm just going to look around and see if maybe this person who chased you left a clue behind."

It's like the tenth time he's called me baby, but I'm too exhausted to scold him about it right now.

"You sound very detective-y right now," I tell him. "It's weird."

"I'm going to take that as a compliment." He winks. "You know, since I know you have a thing for detectives."

I roll my eyes as he reminds me of this crush I had on one of the guys in a mystery book series I became obsessed with freshman year. "That was almost four years ago."

He just smirks, spins around, and begins searching around the area.

Sighing, I return back to painting, trying not to think about how someone could be hiding out in the shadows. I try to tell myself I'm just being paranoid, but in all actuality, I'm not sure I am, especially when West finds something over by the wall that I launched myself over to get away.

"What the hell is this?" he mutters as he crouches down, staring at something shiny and metallic laying on the ground.

As I make my way over to him with the paintbrush clutched in my hand, my heart is a wreck inside my chest. Because, for an instant, the metal object looks like ...

"Is that a knife?" I whisper as I walk up beside West.

Shaking his head, he picks the object up. "No, it's a key." He holds it up in the moonlight to show me.

"It looks old," I remark, reaching out and tracing my finger along the faded, thick metal. "What the heck do you think it goes to?"

He shakes his head as he examines the key. "I have no idea, and maybe it doesn't have to do with any of this."

"Maybe," I agree. "But maybe it does."

He rubs his lips together then straightens. "We'll keep it, just in case." He stuffs it in his pocket and turns toward me. "Are you almost done?" While his question is simple enough, he has this strange, almost horrified look on his face.

Something is wrong.

He's not telling me something.

Does he know what the key is to?

I'm about to ask when he cuts me off.

"Lex." He gives me a pressing. "Aren't you about done painting?"

Yeah, something is definitely up.

"Yeah, pretty much," I tell him as I start back toward the paint bucket. "Just let me clean up."

Relief washes across his features as he nods. "I'll help."

We spend the next ten minutes cleaning up. Then he follows me inside so I can return the painting equipment to the owner and tell him I'm done. West waits for me near the office door while I do.

I expect the store owner to want to go check and make sure I did a good job, but he's busy with a phone call and dismisses me quickly.

When I return to West, we hardly say anything, but we hold hands as we leave the store. Since we drove separate cars, I try to let go of his hand so I can go to mine, but he clutches on to me.

"I'll walk you to your car," he explains with another one of those pressing glances that practically begs me not to argue.

Internally sighing that I have to go against my nature and be cooperative, I nod and let him walk me to my car. When I reach it, I dig out my keys then unlock the door while West glances in the back seat.

"What are you looking for?" I ask as I open the door.

"I'm just making sure everything is safe," he says softly under his breath, his gaze gliding toward me. "I'm going to follow you home, and then we'll talk, okay?"

I bite my bottom lip as I nod. "Okay. But you're really starting to worry me."

"I know. And I'm sorry. I just don't want to talk about this so out in the open."

Anxiousness builds inside me, but I attempt to stifle it.

"All right." I turn to climb in the car, but he cups my jawline and angles my head back toward him.

"See you in a bit," he murmurs then presses his lips against mine. The kiss is brief, and then he's walking away toward his car.

I hurriedly hop into the driver's seat with the imprint of West's lips searing mine.

8

ALEXIS

I'M a bundle of nerves during the drive home, constantly glancing in the back seat, at the sidewalks lining the streets, in my rearview mirror. The sight of West's headlights is the only thing that brings me any sense of comfort in this … whatever this is.

When I pull into the driveaway, Loki's car isn't there. Weird, since he told me via text that he wanted to talk to me.

I check my messages and, sure enough, he sent me one.

Loki: I completely spaced off that Nik had a team BBQ tonight that parents are supposed to go to. I won't be home until around ten, but that doesn't mean we're not going to talk. Either we can do it late tonight or early in the morning. It's your choice.

Great. That means we'll have to wait to ask him about

the papers that West has. I'll make sure it gets done, though. I owe West that much.

I'm actually starting to owe West a lot at this point, something I'm not a huge fan of.

I hate being in debt to people.

Sighing, I climb out of the car right as West parks beside the curb in front of our house. We meet in the middle of the lawn as West pockets his keys.

"Hey, so Loki isn't home," I tell him. "And he won't be home until later—about ten."

West's expression briefly plummets. "I actually have to be somewhere later."

My brows furrow. "Where?"

He scuffs the tip of his boot against the grass while staring down at the road. "Just somewhere."

"Okay …" I drag out the word. "If you don't want to tell me, that's cool." I don't bother pointing out that I've told him a ton of stuff.

I turn to head inside when he folds his fingers around my arm.

"It's not really a big deal," he says. "It's just a house meeting Holden is making us have, and I don't feel like talking about it, because then it reminds me that that's my new home for now."

I twist around to face him. "You wanna …? You wanna sleep on the sofa or something? I'm sure Loki wouldn't mind if you crashed here for a couple of nights."

His gaze carries mine, the corners of his lips quirking. "While I appreciate the offer, Loki's probably got a lot on his plate already, so I think I should probably just stay with Holden and Ellis until I can get my own place." He sketches his fingertip along my cheekbone. "It's cute you're worried about me."

Despite my erratic heartbeat, I narrow my eyes at him, a protest tickling at the tip of my tongue. But I stifle it as someone appears on the sidewalk. It's my neighbor, out walking their dog. Their appearance, though, reminds me of how I had thought I was alone tonight, but I wasn't.

How long was that person watching me in the alleyway before they appeared? Why were they watching me? What were they planning on doing when they caught me?

I gulp as a dark thought creeps into the crevasses of my mind.

What if Jay is the one blackmailing me? And what if he was planning on doing what he did to me that day in the bathroom.

West grazes the back of his hand along my jawline, drawing me from my thoughts. "Let's go inside, okay?" He waits for me to nod then tangles his fingers through mine and steers us toward the front door.

The house is locked up, so I have dig my key out of my pocket. Then, when I open the front door, I have to rush over and turn the alarm off.

"Hello?" I call out, doubting anyone is home since the

lights were off when I entered.

When no one responds, I move past West and lock the front door.

"Let's go up to my room," I tell him. "Just in case someone comes home."

"Afraid someone will see you with me?" he teases.

I shake my head. "Nah. I just don't want anyone overhearing what I need to tell you."

His expression softens, and the look in his eyes is so intense that I have to turn away.

"Come on." I motion for him to follow me as I jog up the stairs.

When we go into my room, I shut the door and toss my keys and phone onto the nightstand, procrastinating as I attempt to figure out what to say.

"It's been a while since I've been in your room," he remarks as he peers around at my mostly bare walls. "It's a lot different."

"I took a lot of my artwork down after my parents passed away," I mumble, glancing at my reflection in the mirror.

Awesome. I look like a hot mess. My hair is tangled, and I somehow got paint on my cheek.

I rub it off with the back of my hand then turn around to tell West what's been going on over the last twenty-four hours, tell him all the stuff I haven't yet, but my heart nearly stops when I see him. Or, well, what he's looking at.

The drawing I did of him last night. And now he's here, staring at it.

"Um … That was for an assignment," I lie, crossing my arms over my chest, feeling exposed at the moment.

He remains silent for a few slamming heartbeats before looking at me. "When did you draw it?"

I want to lie again and plan on doing just that, but when my lips part, the truth falls out.

"Last night, after you dropped me off."

With his lips pressed together, his gaze shifts back to the drawing. "I look sad."

"You looked sad last night when you left," I tell him quietly.

"Did I?" he murmurs then turns to face me. "Why did you draw me?"

"I … I just couldn't get the image of you out of my head, so I drew you because that's what I do. Well, used to do." I'm being way too truthful, and the amount of discomfort rising inside me is making my chest feel pressurized.

And that pressure only magnifies as he steps toward me.

"Lex," he starts.

"Don't," I cut him off, even though I'm unsure what he's going to say. "Don't say anything."

Talking about this … that pressure in my chest … I feel like I'm about to burst open.

He stops in front of me and cups my chin in his hand,

angling my face up toward his. "Okay, I won't," he says, leaning forward and causing me to lean back against the dresser. Then he seals his lips to mine, kissing me. A real kiss. Not one put on for a performance. Just like in his car.

I don't know what to do with that, don't know what to think, so I decide to stop thinking at all and just kiss him back, sliding my arms up his chest and looping them around the back of his neck. He shudders beneath my touching then slides his hand around and tangles his fingers through my hair, tilting my head back even more and kissing me so deeply that I swear my lips are going to bruise. Then he's pulling back, his breath faltering against my face as he keeps his eyes shut, struggling to breathe evenly.

"I … I want to do this right," he whispers, seeming torn about something.

My chest rises and crashes with every ragged breath I take. "Do what right?"

"This." He lifts his eyelids and removes his fingers from my hair, but only to trace them along the side of my face. "You and me."

"I …" I gulp audibly. "I thought we were just pretending?"

"Are we?" He smiles, but nervousness resides in his eyes.

It's time to tell him.

"I have to tell you something. Something the blackmailer did last night."

9

ALEXIS

BY THE TIME I've finished telling West what happened, we're sitting on my bed. He's also gotten very quiet.

"You okay?" I ask after several, quiet minutes tick by.

He nods with a crease between his brow. "Yeah, I'm just trying to figure out what this person wants and why they're going through all this trouble to blackmail people. Not to mention, how in the hell are they getting all these secrets about everyone." He rakes his fingers through his hair, making the strands go askew.

While he hasn't said much, his silence has left a lot of questions hanging between us. Like why he's not trying to deny that he's in love with me.

I absentmindedly trace my fingertip along the pattern of my comforter. "Considering they spied on me while I was sleeping over at your place, they're clearly putting in a lot of effort with this."

He balls his hands into fists. "I'm trying not to think about that part too much, because it makes me want to break something. And threatening to cut your brake cables …" He shakes his head, his jaw ticking. "Maybe we should go to the police."

"No, if we go to the police, then they show everyone those videos of me, and I can't handle that, West. I just can't … I can't think about everyone seeing me like that …" I trail off, working to get air into my lungs.

He cups my face between his hands. "If you don't want to, we won't." He kisses my forehead then leans back and looks me in the eye. "Just take a deep breath, okay?"

Nodding, I do what he says. It's probably the first time I've ever been so cooperative.

Once my breathing has returned to normal, he says cautiously, "I have to tell you something, but before I do, I need to ask you something." A slow breath eases from his lips. "Is the reason why you kissed me in my car today because of what the blackmailer told you to do? Because you made the deal with them about trying to break my heart?"

So, here's the thing; I was too chicken shit to tell him that they also said that he's in love me. Instead, I used the word "like," hoping to make things less awkward. But I still feel like things are awkward. And that awkwardness, I despise it. Part of me wants to lie and say yes so this, this kissing and emotional connection West and I are kind of starting to establish, will end. It might be easier if I just lied. I can be a good liar when I need to. But I'm starting to think that lying is what got me into this blackmailer mess to begin with.

"No," I admit, my heart pounding deafeningly in my chest.

His throat muscles work as he swallows hard . "I didn't kiss you because of the deal, either."

Holy ... Wow ...

Why do I feel so warm right now?

And why do I want to kiss him so badly?

I may have, but he speaks first.

"I talked to Blaine today," he says, nearly giving me whiplash from the subject change.

"Really?" I ask, a little perplexed since the last time they spoke, at least from what I know, West punched Blaine in the face. "Why?"

He lowers his hands from my face and sighs. "Ellis was able to track the number that's been texting you, and it was registered in Blaine's name." So many emotions storm through me, but before I can even attempt to process them, he adds, "He's not sending you the texts, though. He's being blackmailed by the same person, and one of the blackmailer's requests was for him to open a phone line for them. He also ..." He lowers his gaze, staring down at his hands. "It's also why he's been hooking up with Masie."

My eyes widen as I attempt to process everything he's telling me. But it's a lot to take in. These last few days, me getting upset, me ending up with West, has all been because of the blackmailer.

"What dirt does he have on Blaine?" Because, from what I knew, Blaine is a good guy. However, I also thought West was the bad guy, but he's not. At all. Not even a little bit.

"I'm not sure." He lifts his gaze to mine, question marks overflowing from his eyes. Although, I don't know what he's confused about. "He wouldn't tell me, but he was acting really paranoid when I went to talk to him. He even made me drive up to our spot by the lake so he could be positive no one was following us. I guess the blackmailer somehow found out we were together, though, and they told him that he had to beat my ass, or else they'd out whatever they have over him."

"*What*? He beat you up because of that?"

"I told him to," he clarifies, lightly touching the wound on his forehead. "Not that I'm still not pissed off at him, but he looked so freaked out that my dumbass felt sorry for him."

"You're not dumb. You were being a good friend." I pause. "He has no idea who's doing this?"

"No, but I find it strange that both you and Blaine are getting blackmailed by them, since you two are close.

Makes me wonder if perhaps you both know who the person is."

"Blaine and I *were* close," I stress. "I feel like I don't even know him anymore. And honestly, I don't think he knows me anymore either."

He observes me closely, uncertainty written all over his face. I'm about to ask him what the hell is up with that look when he asks, "Now that you know he's not really into Masie, does that …?" He huffs out frustrated exhale. "Do you think you'll be friends with him again?"

I shrug. "I have no idea."

And I really don't.

I also don't think he really meant to use the word *friends.*

He wants to know if I like Blaine again now that I know the truth—that Blaine isn't really into Masie. But through all this—me seeing him kiss Masie, me cutting that tie with him—it made me realize that I'm unsure if I even still liked Blaine, that maybe I was just latching on to that love I once felt for him, because it made me feel connected to my past when my parents were alive still. And I was telling the truth when I told West that Blaine and I don't really know each other anymore. Truthfully, West probably knows more about me right now than Blaine does. What that means, though, I haven't got a clue. Or maybe I do and am just afraid to let myself admit it aloud.

"So, about that key you found in the alley," I say, deflecting. "What do you think that's for?"

He stares at me with an unreadable expression, probably because he can totally tell that I'm avoiding having a conversation about Blaine. Still, he lets me off the hook, digging the key out of his pocket.

"I'm not sure. Maybe it doesn't even have anything to do with the person in the hoodie, but it did seem weirdly out of place." He holds the key in the palm of his hand, examining it.

I lean toward him to get a better look. Under the light, I can see how old it is, rusted around the edges and bulky. But what is really strange is the markings engraved into the top.

"What do you think these are?" I ask, running my fingertip along the markings.

"I'm not sure, but I don't think they're just random scratches."

"Yeah, they look like symbols."

Biting his bottom lip, he glances up at me. "Tonight, do you think you could draw that tattoo you saw on that guy's neck? Then, maybe tomorrow, I can have Ellis run image searches on that and these markings."

I nod. "I can do that." At least, I hope I can.

I haven't tried to draw anything else since the drawing of West. And when I did that, I was in some sort of emotional, overpowering state. But drawing a tattoo doesn't have to mean anything. It's just a simple drawing; that's all.

"I also don't want to be all weird or anything," West says cautiously, "but I think you should be careful for a bit and maybe try not to be alone as much as possible."

"I get why you're saying that, and I understand that I probably should, but I also don't have a lot of people in my life that I'm close to."

He tucks a strand of my hair behind my ear. "You have me."

God, I really wish he'd stop saying stuff like that. And looking me like he thinks I'm important. And touching me so gently, so carefully.

"You can't be with me twenty-four seven," I remind him.

"Says who?" he teases.

"Says life," I quip. "You have your own life, your own stuff going on. You can't just spend all your time with me."

"Maybe not *all* my time, although it'd be sort of fun." He grins amusedly. "We could sleep in the same bed, all pressed up together. And then, when we wake up, we could share the shower." When I narrow my eyes at him, he gives me an innocent look. "Only to save water. I like to do my part in trying to help the environment."

I bite back a smile as I shake my head, and a smile takes over his face. But underneath the smile, he looks worn out with bags under his eyes and that cut on his forehead hasn't been properly cleaned yet.

He has so much to deal with as it is already, and yet he's here, with me, helping me out with my own shit.

"We should go clean up your cut," I tell him, lightly brushing my finger just below the wound.

His smile fizzles as he smashes his lips together. "Okay." His voice sounds hoarse, but I'm not sure why, other than maybe my touching him hurt.

Lowering my hand, I climb off the bed and start for the door. He follows me, resting his hand on my lower back. I could step out of his touch—it's not like we need to pretend that we're dating right now—but I find myself comforted by the gesture.

West, he's really been there for me through all this.

And he's not who I thought he was.

He's sweet and kind and, yes, I'll admit, sexy.

And his kisses …

Wow …

"You okay?" he asks as we enter the small bathroom. "You seem kind of tense."

"I'm just peachy," I lie as I collect the first-aid kit from under the sink. Then I stand up and pat the counter. "Hop up. I'll patch you up."

With the corners of his lips tilted upward, he hoists himself onto the counter. "Aw, you gonna play doctor for me? If so, you should go put on a naughty nurse's outfit."

I make a big show of rolling my eyes as I open the kit and move in front of him.

My heart is a mess as I imagine doing what he's implying. I wouldn't even know how to do that—be sexy— because I'm completely inexperienced and West isn't. I know that for a fact.

"I don't have one," I say. "And besides, nurses wear scrubs."

"True." He watches me intently as I get out the peroxide and a cotton ball. "For Halloween, you should dress up as one. You'd look sexy as hell."

"Nah, that's not really my style." I set the kit down on the counter. "Maybe you can convince Stella Mafelerton to do it for you, though."

He angles his head to the side. "What the hell does Stella Mafelerton have to do with this?"

I douse the cotton ball with peroxide. "Today, I heard her talking about how hot she thinks you are. If you go to that party this weekend, you might get lucky."

Amusement glitters in his eyes. "Wouldn't that be a little weird, since *you* are my girlfriend?"

"Fake girlfriend." I set the bottle of peroxide down. "And we never established how long we are gonna date. We could always break up before the party"

"Yeah, we never did establish a timeframe, did we?" His gaze burrows into me as I lift my hand and dab his wound with the cotton ball. He winces then clears his throat. "Lex … about what the blackmailer told you."

I cringe as my hand noticeably trembles. "Which part?"

He circles his fingers around my wrists, searing hot, drawing my attention to him. "About me liking you." He rubs his lips together then lowers my hand from his wound. "It's true. I've liked you for a while."

Hearing him say it aloud almost makes my heart jolt, and I end up dropping the cotton ball.

"Are you being seriously right now?" I question skeptically as I pick up the cotton ball and set it down on the counter.

"Don't act like that, Lex. Like there's no way I could possibly like you. You're gorgeous as hell, smart, sarcastic, funny, sweet, even though you pretend not to be, and talented. You're also feisty when you need to be."

"I'm also a pain in the ass." I joke in an attempt to mask what his words are doing to me.

I feel like I'm about to crawl out of my skin and all that's left will be bones, cracked bones, and a splintered heart, and he'll see it all.

"Yeah, that, too," he agrees with a nervous grin. "But it doesn't change how I feel."

Oh my God, I think he's actually being serious. But how? And …

"For … For how long?"

"How long have I liked you?" he asks, and I nod. He gives a half-shrug, but the move is a bit stiff. "For a while."

He's nervous about telling me this. Why? Because he's putting himself out there? Or is it because of something else?

For a while?

How ...?

What?

My lips part in shock. "But you never said anything."

"I know. Because I knew you were in love with Blaine," he stresses with a pressing look.

My lips form an O.

Silence stretches between us, and the awkwardness builds.

"It's okay if you don't feel the same way." He forces a fake smile onto his face. "We can just be friends, if that's what you want."

What the hell do I want? I'm not sure.

Clueless Alexis. I know her really well.

But that doesn't mean I just want to stay friends with West. Not when I like kissing him. Not after everything that he's done for me. And if I'm being really honest with myself, hearing him confess that he likes me is making my heart act like a total nutjob.

West likes me. Gorgeous, flirty West, who beautiful girls like Stella get crushes on.

"I don't know how you can like me." The words just sort

of tumble out of my mouth. "I mean, I know you said all of those things, but I'm a mess, and I'm not … I'm just …" I take a deep breath as Jay's words pierce through my mind.

You're a freak.

Ugly.

No one wants you.

I hate that I can't shake his words.

Hate him for making me hate myself.

"Hey." He grabs my waist and pulls me forward until I'm standing between his legs. "You're all the things I said and more. And I don't know what happened to you, although that fucking video gives me a bit of insight"—his tone briefly quivers with rage, but he quickly collects himself —"but all the things I said, I meant. You are all those things, and I really do like you, a fucking ton."

He likes me a fucking ton?

West? My frenemy? Well, my friend now … fake boyfriend … the guy I like …

We really need to figure out what we are, I think.

"I like you, too." I guess that might be a start.

"Yeah?" he asks with a crooked smile, and I give an unsteady nod, feeling like that wall I built around me cracked apart. He releases the most relieved breath I've ever heard then slants toward me, tracing his thumb along my bottom lip. "I'm going to kiss you, okay? And it's going to be a fucking real kiss—a true one. I want to make sure you understand that."

I want to say something epic, but I'm way too erratic of a mess right now to form comprehendible words, so I just nod.

He wets his lips with his tongue then leans in to kiss me, shutting his eyes. So I do mine. The moment his lips touch mine, I swear to God sparks sizzle around me.

Zap.

My eyelids shoot open just in time to see the lightbulbs flicker on and off. Then darkness encases us.

West jerks back from me. "Shit." He gently guides me back then lowers himself from the counter, his hand finding mine. "Are you okay?"

"Yeah … But what happened?" I ask. "Was that like a power outage or something?"

"I have no idea." He holds my hand while digging his phone out of his pocket. He turns on the flashlight app and light pierces the darkness. "I want you to stay here," he says, giving my hand a squeeze. "Lock the door until I come back. You have your phone on you, right?"

"Yes, but … West …" The protest fades as he wiggles his hand from mine and strides toward the door "West," I hiss, trailing after him. "I don't think you should go out there."

Not that I'm entirely convinced we should be concerned about the power going off. Maybe there was a power shortage. Or maybe the bulb just burnt out and the rest of the lights in the house will work. Then again, I have a sinking feeling in the pit of my stomach that I can't shake, like a warning flag. This has happened to me before, and one time in particular was right before my parents were in that car accident.

Maybe I should tell them not to go, I thought after a nightmare I'd had.

But I didn't tell them to …

"Please don't go." I stumble over to him and clutch his arm. "Or let me come with you at least."

He turns to look at me, his face just a shadow in the dark. "I don't … It makes me nervous—you being out there when we're not sure if there's someone here."

"I know." I briefly pause. "But the same thing makes me nervous for you."

His cheeks puff as he blows out a breath. "I … Fine. We'll both go out there, but just keep ahold of my hand and hold on to your phone in case we need to call the cops."

Nodding, I retrieve my phone from my pocket then thread my fingers with his.

"You ready?" he asks, although he doesn't sound ready himself.

"Yeah." It's probably the biggest lie I've ever told.

1 0

WEST

SHE'S BUSTING WITH ANXIETY, and I hate it. Hate that this blackmailer has got her so wound up that she's giving herself anxiety. It pisses me off, although not as much as when she told me about what happened in the alleyway. No, the level of rage I feel toward that is almost as potent as when I saw that video of what Jay did to her.

I'm going to figure this out for her.

And I'm going to protect her.

I just hope I can keep my own life together while I do.

"You doing okay?" I ask Lex as we make our way down the dark hallway and toward the stairway.

I have the flashlight on my phone on and am sweeping it from left to right as we walk, edginess rippling through me. Part of me wants to call the cops, but we don't really have a reason to right now. And I hope it stays that way.

Hope this is just a power outage. But with everything going on, I can't look at things that way—

The lights suddenly turn back on, and I have to blink several times for my eyes to readjust to the light. Then I turn off my flashlight and twist to face Lex. She's rubbing her eyes with her free hand, her other hand clutching onto mine with the phone between our palms. She has a few droplets of paint splatters across her cheeks and in her hair. The sight of it reminds me of when she used to be really into art and would always have paint or charcoal on her.

I thought she had stopped drawing and painting. Then I saw that drawing of me that captured the pain I was feeling so perfectly that it was alarming. I might have ended up feeling those emotions all over again just looking at that drawing, but the fact that she drew me had me so distracted.

Lex drew me. Me. Not Blaine.

"I guess it was just a power shortage," Lex says, drawing me from my thoughts.

"I guess so." Unable to help myself, I reach forward and rub at the spots of paint on her cheeks.

A crinkle forms between her brows. "What're you doing?"

"You have paint on your cheeks," I tell her with a smile. "It's cute how it's all splattered amongst your freckles."

She crinkles her nose. "My freckles aren't cute."

"No, they're fucking adorable." I slowly back her up against the wall and cup her chin in my hand. "The power outrage ruined my kiss."

She nervously wets her lips with her tongue. "I know."

I skim my thumb along her jawline. "And I want to finish it so you know I'm being serious about this."

"That you …? That you want to kiss me?"

"And date you." I move my thumb to her bottom lip. "For reals. Not fake."

"And … And what about what the blackmailer wants me to do?"

"That can be an added bonus to us dating. We can play the blackmailer with this. Make him think that you're playing me, but it can be real." I smile at her, waiting for her to agree, but when she doesn't, my smile fades into apprehension. "Unless you don't want to."

"No … I think I do … I mean, I do … I just …" She grimaces. "I'm just a little bit nervous about this. I mean, everything is so new to me, and I don't really know what I'm doing. And you do. And I …" She blows out a frustrated sigh. "I'm not Stella Mafelerton."

"I know you're not." My brows knit. "Why are you pointing that out?"

She continues to grow more frustrated. "Stella Mafelerton is experienced and knows what she's doing, like you do. And I just had my first kiss, like, a few days ago, which you know since you're the one who kissed me."

"Again, I know all of this," I tell her, confused. "What I don't get is why you're saying all this stuff."

"I just think …" Her gaze wanders up to the ceiling as she shakes her head and takes a deep breath. "You're experienced, and I'm not. And if we dated, we'd have to go kind of slow since I'm still working on stuff. Plus, with everything going on, I don't want to make things more complicated."

I relax a smidgeon. "Lex, what did you think I meant earlier when I said I want to do this right?"

She shrugs, her gaze returning to mine, confusion filling her eyes. "I have no idea."

I sweep a strand of her hair out of her face. "I meant that I want to do this right with you. I don't want to just hook up. Trust me; I've waited a while for things to happen between us. I'm not going to risk screwing it up by rushing into anything."

"So … So, you don't want to have sex, then?" she asks, her cheeks flushing.

Jesus, that blush. Lex rarely blushes, but I really wish she would more, because it's the most adorable thing I've ever seen.

I nibble on my bottom lip, choosing my next words carefully. "No, that's not what I'm saying. I do want to have sex with you. I'm just saying that we can take things slow." As her cheeks turn even more pink, I can't help smiling. "You're blushing."

"No, I'm not," she scoffs.

"Yeah, you are."

"Yeah, well … you're saying you want to have sex with me, so I don't know what you expect."

"I don't expect anything. That's what I'm trying to say." I swallow hard as I prepare to put a truth out there between us. "But I do want you, like, a lot. I've fucking fantasized about it for a while now."

Her breathing starts to quicken. I think she is freaking out, but she's looking me in the eye, not somewhere else like she would be if she was contemplating running.

"I'm going to kiss you now, okay?" My voice is a lot more wobbly than I want it to be.

She bobs her head up and down, quiet breaths rushing from her lips. "Okay."

My own breathing starts to pick up as I lean in. With how worked up we both are, I know that, when we kiss, it's going to be intense. But even knowing that doesn't prepare me for the intensity that pulsates through me when my lips touch hers.

I groan as desire courses through me, and I let my hands drift to her waist, holding her up. Or maybe I'm trying to hold myself up. Who the hell knows and who the hell cares? All I know is that I want this. Want her.

"You okay with this?" I double-check, my lips hovering a sliver of an inch away from hers.

"Yeah," she breathes out, moving her hands to the hem of my shirt.

As she clutches onto the fabric, her fingers graze across the skin of my waist. Desire ripples through me, and I kiss her deeply, our tongues tangling.

My hands unconsciously wander up and down her sides as I work to keep us both upright. I'm trying to go slow, to keep control of myself, but the longer we kiss, the quicker our movements become. And when she leans against the wall behind her and hitches her leg around my waist, I damn near lose it.

I grind my hips against hers, and she moans, digging her fingers into my sides. I just about pull back, not wanting to push her, when she rolls her hips against mine. We did this a little bit in my car in the school parking lot, but this feels different, maybe because I made it pretty clear we're not pretending.

This is real, and Lex knows it. And she's not pulling away.

But I also told her I'd take things slow, and this doesn't feel slow. So, instead of rocking my hips against hers again, I focus on kissing her, focus on letting my hands travel up and down her sides, along her arms, the sides of her neck.

Her skin is so soft, and she tastes like cherries. I want to taste her everywhere. But I'm not going to yet. I'm not going to screw this up like I've done with everything else in my life. So, I keep kissing her, tasting her lips and feeling her skin. And nothing exists in that moment. Not my parents. Not those papers. Not the drug deals waiting for me when I leave. It's just Lex and me here. And if I could, I would stay this way for a while. And maybe I would've if the house alarm didn't go off, letting us know someone is here.

That we're no longer alone.

ALEXIS

I THINK I might really be starting to like this whole kissing thing. Like a freakin' ton. Although, I wonder if I'd like it as much if I wasn't kissing West. I honestly don't think so. Not with how easy falling into kissing him is.

Not that the kissing isn't intense. It's beyond tense. Blazing. Full of heat. I can't believe I haven't been doing this for longer.

I probably would've kissed him all night if the house alarm hadn't gone off.

Panic soars through me and yanks me out of my kissing-West daze. He tenses, too, as his lips leave mine.

His lips part. "Who do you—"

"Nik, can you turn off the alarm?" Loki calls out.

I relax.

"It's Loki and Nik," I state the obvious. Although,

they're earlier than Loki said. "We should go have Loki look at those papers."

Nodding, he moves to step back, but then he dips his head and kisses me again.

"I just wanted one more," he explains then moves back, smiling at me.

I try to smile back, but I'm sure I look like a riled-up freak with how fast my heart is sprinting. Then I head down the hallway with him trailing at my heels.

Right before I start down the stairs, he grabs my hand and stops me.

"Your brother's not going to, like, freak out that we were here alone, is he?" he asks, scratching the back of his neck.

I shrug. "I don't know. I've never really been in this situation before. And besides, as far as Loki knows, we're just friends. Or, well, frenemies," I joke, but he doesn't even so much as smile. "Dude, why are you so stressed out about this?"

He gives a stiff shrug. "I don't know. Adults just don't seem to like me very much. And I want your family to like me."

"Well, Zhara likes you, so you've won one person over already," I tell him. "Nik's going through his teenage angst phase, so he doesn't even like *me* right now. Anna is ... Well, I don't really know what's going on with her, but I doubt she'd judge you since she's had to deal with being judged harshly before. And Loki's barely an adult, so you don't really need to worry about him. Honestly, it's me he doesn't really like right now."

"Yeah, but—"

I cover his mouth with my hand. "No buts. You'll be fine. Just be yourself." When I lower my hand, he cracks a smile.

Finally.

"You're acting like being myself is a good thing," he says.

I roll my eyes. "We both know that you can be super charming when you want to be."

He muses over that. "True. I did charm you over."

I roll my eyes again, this time way more dramatically. "Come on; let's go talk to him about those papers."

He follows me, growing quiet again, and part of me wants to reach back and hold his hand. But the other part of me realizes that right now might not be the best time to declare my relationship status to Loki, considering I was home alone with West and am clearly coming from the direction of my bedroom.

"Lex, is that you?" Loki calls out as I reach the bottom of the stairway.

"Yeah." I head for the kitchen with West right behind me.

When I enter, Nik is digging through the fridge and Loki is rummaging through a takeout bag that's on the counter.

"I picked you, Zhara, and Anna some food up for dinner," Loki says without glancing up at me. "Nik and I ate at the BBQ, but I got myself some dessert so we can sit down, eat, and talk ..." He trails off as he glances up at me. Well, glances up at me and West, since his gaze is currently bouncing back and forth between us.

He probably thinks I brought him home with me to get out of talking to him, so I hurriedly tell him what's going on. "I'm going to sit down with you and eat and talk about all the things I know I messed up with," I inform him. "But there's this thing going on with West that we're really hoping you can help us out with."

Puzzlement creases his features. "Okay, what is it?"

I turn to West. "You wanna go grab those papers?"

West nods, glancing at Loki nervously before heading toward the front door.

Niki exits the kitchen, too, stuffing his face with a handful of chips.

The moment both of them walk out, Loki says to me, "West hasn't been over here in a while."

I shrug, wandering from the doorway and into the kitchen. "It's not like we were super close friends."

He gives me a funny look as he rests his arms on the counter of the kitchen island, looking at me. "Maybe you don't see it that way."

I stop on the other side of the counter. "What does that mean?"

He wavers with his lips pressed together, his gaze traveling to the doorway then back to me. "It means that he likes you as more than a friend."

While I know that, I'm not sure … "How do you know that?"

He lifts a shoulder as he stands upright again. "About a year ago, he was over here. Blaine and Masie were here, too. You guys were working on some group project. Anyway, you and West were arguing about something—I honestly can't even remember. What I do remember is the way he was looking at you when you weren't paying attention to him."

"How was he looking at me?"

"Like he wanted to be looking at you," he explains. "I remember because it made me nervous."

I'm taken back by the statement. "Why did it make you nervous?"

He shrugs. "Because it made me realize that, eventually, I was going to have to deal with you, Zhara, and Anna dating."

"Oh." I'm not sure how to deal with that. And I don't have to since he continues.

"Plus, back then, everyone in this family knew you had a crush on Blaine."

"*What*? No, they didn't."

"Yeah, they did. Mom and Dad used to talk about sometimes. They weren't really fans of you liking him."

My confusion magnifies. "They weren't?"

He nods. "I'm not sure if you still like him that way—you're more harder to read these days—and I'm not positive why Mom and Dad didn't like Blaine, but I do know that I was a teenage guy once and spent a lot of time hanging out with teenage guys that were like Blaine, and trust me, it's better if you just let that crush stay a crush."

"Is this your way of trying to give me dating advice?" I question, because that's new.

He wavers. "If I had my way, none of you girls would date until you were, like, twenty-five, but I'm also not stupid enough to believe that'll happen, so all I can do is give you some advice. Blaine won't be good for you. At least, not right now. Maybe when he's older, but that depends on how much he changes."

"Okay." I give a considering pause. "What about West?"

"Hmm ..." he mutters. "Is there an option C, where no guy has to be in the equation?"

"No, I'm not a nun."

"You could be, if you wanted to," he says. When I narrow my eyes at him, he laughs. "Fine. West is fine. At least, he's better than Blaine. But let's just leave the nun idea out there, okay?"

I start to roll my eyes when the front door opens.

I quickly clear my throat and give Loki a pressing look, urging him to please stop talking about boyfriends and nuns.

He just chuckles under his breath, which annoys me, but at least he seems to be in a decent mood. I wonder why, since we're supposed to be talking about how I got detention at school.

Maybe he doesn't know why.

I don't really get a chance to ask him either since West walks in with the folder of papers in his hands. His eyes immediately stray in Loki's direction before settling on me.

"Here they are," he tells me, anxiety evident in his tone.

Is he anxious over the papers or Loki? It's really hard to tell. And Loki isn't making it easier as he puts his humor aside and goes into formal mode.

"So, what're in these papers that I'm supposed to be looking at?" he asks as he picks up the takeout bag and makes his way over to the table.

West's Adam's apple bobs as he swallows. "Um … They're these papers that I took from Eli—my dad …" He huffs out a frustrated exhale.

"They're these papers that Eli, who's supposed to be his dad, tried to make him sign," I chime in for him, offering him a small I-got-this smile. Then I take the folder from him and set it down in front of Loki as he takes a seat at the table.

His forehead furrows. "Supposed to be his dad?"

I nod, taking a seat at the table and signaling for West to come sit down, too. Then the two of us give Loki a recap of what happened today. Well, minus anything that has to do with the blackmailer.

While we talk, we eat. Since Loki bought extra food, West eats with us.

During the half an hour conversation, I think about my parents a few times, remembering how my family would eat dinner around the table. This may not be the exact situation, but I find a bit of comfort in it. If only we weren't talking about how West's fake parents are practically trying to screw him out of his inheritance.

"A guy I went to school with is a lawyer," Loki says once we finish explaining everything to him. "If you want, I can call him up and see if he can look into this."

West pops a fry into his mouth. "Is he from Honeyton?"

Loki shakes his head as he takes a sip of his drink. "No. He lives in Fareland. And he's pretty trustworthy."

West nods, wiping his fingers onto a napkin. "All right. Thanks."

"No problem. I'll call him tomorrow and let Lex know what I find out." Loki rises to his feet, collects the folder of papers, and looks at me. "I have some inventory to fill out for the store, so I'll be up in my room. Once you're finished with dinner, come up so we can talk about what happened at school, okay?"

Le sigh. Somehow, in the midst of everything tonight, I managed to conveniently forget that I got detention.

I dunk a fry into a cup of fry sauce. "Okay."

"And make sure it's sooner rather than later," he warns then walks out of the kitchen, leaving West and me alone.

I stuff the fry into my mouth then wipe the grease off my fingertips. "Do you feel any better now?"

West is staring at the table but shifts his gaze to me and nods. "Actually, I kind of do. Thanks." A small smile graces his lips, and then he leans across the table and lightly brushes his lips across mine. He tastes like salty fries, but that's okay. I probably do, too. "Thank you for doing that," he tells me as he slants back.

"Of course." I smile at him. "What're friends for?"

"You're better than all my friends, Lex," he says in all seriousness. "I wouldn't even trust anyone else with this information."

My mind fleeting wanders back to what Loki said, how he's known for a while that West likes me simply because of the way he was looking at me. If that's true, how did I not see it? Because I was so blinded by my crush on Blaine?

Man, if that's true, then talk about pathetic.

Ping.

West's phone goes off, startling us both. Rubbing his hand across his forehead, he digs his phone out of his pocket and reads the message. I notice a visible change in his expression as he does, his features tightening, the corners of his lips tilting downward.

"Is everything okay?" I ask.

He nods, pocketing his phone. "I'm just supposed to be somewhere, so I need to go."

I eye him over, unsure if he's being truthful or not. "Are you sure that's it?"

He offers me a forced smile. "Of course." Then he pushes the chair back from the table and rises to his feet.

I stand up, too. "Was the message from Loraine and Eli?"

Wisps of his hair fall into his eyes as he shakes his head. "I blocked their number for now."

"Oh. That's probably a good idea." But that also leaves me questioning who texted him something that made his mood plummet.

Maybe I'm just overthinking this? Maybe the black-mailer is making me a worrier? Maybe I need to chill out?

But, as I walk him to the door with silence building between us, worry continues to stir through me.

Something's wrong.

However, I don't know how to get the truth out of him.

He wraps his fingers around the doorknob then pauses and turns to me. "You want to ride with me to school tomorrow?"

"Sure."

His frown morphs into a smile, but he doesn't say anything.

"What's that look for?" I wonder.

He rolls his tongue in his mouth. "It's nothing."

"No, it's clearly something." I cross my arms and stare him down. "So spit it out, dude."

"It really is nothing," he assures me. "I was just thinking about how you didn't even have to think about it when I asked you, which means you're starting to like me."

I hold up my hand with my finger and thumb a sliver of an inch apart. "Maybe just a tiny bit."

His smile widens. "Liar." Then he dips his head and kisses me, surprising me so much that I stumble and grab his arms for support. "I'll see you tomorrow morning," he whispers against my lips. Then he moves back, smiling at me one final time before walking out the door.

I work to get my breathing under control, something his kiss did. Then I start to lock up the house. As I'm setting the alarm, though, it dawns on me that Zhara isn't home yet.

I take out my phone and send her a text.

Me: Where are you?

Zhara: I'm hanging out with Benton. Why? Is something wrong?

Me: No. I was just wondering where you were.

Zhara: Oh, okay. Well, I'll be home in an hour.

Me: Okay. Have fun. ;)

I put the phone away and slowly make my way up to Loki's bedroom. When I enter, he's lounging on the bed with papers scattered around him. I knock on the doorframe so he knows I'm there. When he glances up at me with a frown on his face, I expect him to go straight into a lecture about getting detention. But he doesn't.

"Lex, I don't want you getting involved in this thing with Loraine and Eli," he says as he sets the paper he's holding down.

"I'm not really involved," I inform him. "I'm just helping West out."

"I know, but …" He removes his glasses, sets them down on the nightstand, and then scoots to the edge of the bed, lowering his feet to the floor. "I don't want you getting involved in anything that has to do with them. Those two aren't the kind of people you want to get mixed up with; trust me. They will destroy your life if they feel like you're threatening theirs in any way."

"How …? Why are you saying this?"

"Because I'm trying to protect you."

"You're being vague."

"I know. And I'm sorry about that. For now, I just need you to trust me on this."

Confusion webs through me. "What about West? We said we'd help him."

"And we're going to," he assures, "by giving these papers to my lawyer friend and letting him handle this the legal way."

"You're keeping something from me," I state with annoyance.

"I know. And I wish I didn't have to, but for now, it's for

the best. Maybe one day, after this is all taken care of, I'll tell you. To protect you, I'm going to keep what I know to myself." He offers me an apologetic look.

"Does this …? Does this have to do with West, too?"

"No, just Loraine and Eli. Like I said, I have nothing against West." He loosens his tie. "In fact, after seeing you with him at dinner, I'm kind of glad you're hanging out with him."

"Really?" I ask in doubt.

"Yes, really." His brow arches. "Should I not be glad?"

I push away from the doorframe. "No. I'm just wondering what you saw that made you think that."

He pulls off his tie. "You seemed lighter."

"I did?"

"Yeah." He tosses his tie onto the bed. "And while I don't want to put more heaviness on you, we need to talk about what happened at school." He crosses his arms. "Why did you cut class?"

I crinkle my nose. "I wasn't really cutting class. I was just late."

"Yeah, but why?"

"Because I needed to talk to West about something— something private—and he wanted to talk about those papers, so we went out to his car, and the conversation ended up going for longer than I expected." I offer him the partial truth, not wanting to tell him about how I made out with West after the conversation.

He rubs his hand over his jawline. "What did you need to talk to him about?"

I shrug. "A bunch of drama that's going on between Masie, Blaine, and me."

He eyes me over. "What sort of drama?"

I grimace. "Masie and Blaine are dating, and Masie knew I liked Blaine, so it kind of feels like she stabbed me in the back, especially because Masie told Blaine that I liked him."

He hesitates. "Can I be real with you for a moment?"

I nod. "I'd rather you be real than lie."

He slants forward and rests his arms on his legs. "I've never thought Masie was a good friend to you. She always treated you so poorly. So, while I wish I could say this is a surprise, it's not. And I also hope that maybe after this, you'll let the friendship fade out."

"It's already faded," I assure him. "Although, that kind of leaves me friendless."

"You're not friendless. You have your brothers and sisters. And I know for a fact Zhara would love for you two to be close again." He fleetingly pauses. "It also looks like you have West. Though, no more hanging out in your bedroom while no one's home, okay?" He gives me a firm look.

I give him a salute. "Yes, boss."

He rolls his eyes but smiles. "I'm not going to ground you for getting detention, but only because you've been behaving better over the last handful of days. As long as you keep it up, I think having detention is punishment enough."

He's letting me off the hook? Seriously?

"Okay … Thanks." I'm so confused, but it's not like I'm going to argue.

"How did painting the store go today?" he asks as he turns back to the papers on his bed.

"It was fine. The owner wasn't a total douchebag, so that's a plus."

"Good. I just hope you learned your lesson."

"I did," I promise. In more ways than I can ever explain.

The last thing I ever want is to put myself in another situation where this blackmailer can get more dirt on me. Or where they can corner me in an alleyway and try to scare the crap out of me.

"I hope so," he mumbles, getting distracted by his papers. "I want to start having family dinners again. I also think you and I should set a time and date when we can sit down and discuss what you want to do after graduation."

Ugh, the dreaded *G* word. It'd be fine, except I have no clue what I want to do.

I chew on my thumbnail. "What if I don't know what I want to do?"

"That's fine. Maybe us talking about it will help give you some ideas."

"Um … Okay." Doubtful. But again, I'm not about to argue.

I start to walk out of the room to go take a shower, do my homework, and then attempt to draw that tattoo I saw on that guy's neck.

"And Lex?" Loki calls out, causing me to pause. "Thanks for talking to me and for … well, being cooperative about this."

"Thanks for not grounding me. And for fixing my car."

"That's what I'm here for." He wavers. "Well, I'll still ground you if I need to."

I laugh softly then walk out of the room. I grab some clothes, take a quick shower, and then get set up in my bed with my pencils and sketchbook. I've just drawn the first line when someone knocks on my door.

"Come in," I call out as I draw another line while attempting to visualize the tattoo on the guy's neck.

"Hey," Zhara greets as she walks into my room.

"Hey," I reply, setting the pencil and sketchbook down on the bed.

Her gaze tracks the movements then her brows rise in surprise. "You're drawing again?"

I give a dismissive shrug. "Not really. I just saw this tattoo today that looked kind of cool, so I'm trying to draw it."

"Oh." She drums her fingers against the sides of her legs. "Are you getting a tattoo?"

"Not now. Maybe one day, though." I scoot to the edge of the bed. "I'm just drawing it up so West can see it."

"West, huh?" Interest sparkles in her eyes. "I heard a rumor around school that you two are dating. Is that the fake dating think you were telling me about?"

I scratch my arm. "No ..."

"So, you guys are really dating now?"

I nod.

"Really?" A smile breaks across her face. "I knew it."

"Knew what?"

"That he liked you."

"Since when?"

"Since forever."

I gape at her. "Why does everyone in this house keep saying this?"

She laughs, stepping farther into my room. "Because every time West would come over, it was pretty clear he liked you. He always would stare at you and flirt with you."

"He didn't flirt with me," I correct. "He teased me and annoyed the crap out of me."

"He teased/flirted with you," she insists. "Like when we were in grade school and Jay would pull your hair because he had a crush on you." I try to keep my expression neutral at her mention of Jay, but I must fail since she says, "What's wrong?"

"It's nothing," I say with a shrug. "I just don't like Jay."

"I don't blame you. He's kind of an ... asshole now."

Despite the heavy conversation, despite the emotions stewing inside me, I can't help myself. I bust up laughing.

"Did you just swear?"

"I …" Puzzlement creases her features. "I didn't, did I?"

"You totally did." I rein in on my laughter the best that I can. "I seriously can't remember the last time I heard you swear."

"Yeah, well…" She exhales exhaustedly. "I was hanging out with Benton and his band today, and they've all got filthy mouths. I think I must've picked up on it or something." She looks guilty for a moment.

"Zee, you don't need to feel guilty for swearing. It's perfectly okay not to be perfect all the time. Not that swearing is even bad. You just have it in your head that it is."

"I know," she admits. "I'm just … I'm trying to figure out who I am and it's hard."

Story of my damn life. "I get that."

"Yeah?"

"Yeah." I crisscross my legs. "So, are you gonna do this whole road trip, fake dating thing?"

"I think so. I mean, Loki didn't completely say yes yet, but he also didn't say no either."

"He seemed super chill tonight. Maybe you should try to get a confirmed answer from him now."

"Okay. Yeah, I'll do that." She spins around to walk out, but then she turns right back around. "Actually, I almost forgot the reason I came in here. I need to borrow an outfit from you, if you're okay with that?"

I lift a shoulder. "Sure. But why?" I glance at her shorts, pink shirt, and strappy sandals get-up. "My clothes are definitely not your style."

"That's kind of the point," she explains. "I need to look more rebellious, so I'll look like I'm actually someone Benton would date."

Irritation bites through me. "Did he say that to you? Because if he did, I don't think you should do this."

She swiftly shakes his head. "No, Benton's been really nice to me, Lex, I promise. But we talked about it, and if I'm going to fit in with the band's image, I need to dress differently." She shifts her weight and wraps her arms around herself. "Plus, I know that no one would look at me right now and think someone like Benton would be interested in me."

That irritation stirs. "You need to stop thinking like that. You're smart, good at a ton of things, nice, and pretty. And don't think otherwise." When she doesn't say anything right away, I add, "You have to think you're pretty because we're twins, so if you think you're ugly, it means you think I'm ugly."

"We're not identical."

"So? We look similar."

She considers what I said. "I don't think I'm ugly, but I still want to borrow an outfit of yours. And not because

I'm changing myself for Benton. I'm honestly just trying to figure out who *I* am."

"You said that already," I mutter. "It's weird because I always thought you knew who you were. In fact, sometimes I felt jealous of it."

"We're almost eighteen, Lex. No one at eighteen really knows who they are. But it's definitely the perfect time to start figuring it out."

She's right.

She really is.

But, unlike her, I don't know where to start.

"I'm going to go talk to Loki. Then will you help me pick out an outfit?" she asks with hope in her eyes.

While I'm a little bit wary of her changing herself for this band/fake dating thing, I manage to smile. "Sure."

She smiles brightly at me in return. "Thanks." Then she practically skips out the door.

While I'm glad she's not acting like the perfect, borderline robotic Zhara, I worry about her. She hasn't experienced a lot of things in her life, at least as far as I know, and she sometimes has a naïve way of looking at things.

I'll just have to make sure to keep an eye on her. And when she goes on the road with the band ... well, I need to figure out a way to stay in touch with her. Then again, maybe I'm the wrong person to do that, considering the current status on my life.

Blowing out a loud exhale, I pick up my sketchbook and

pencil. Then I spend the next thirty minutes or so trying to recaptures the tattoo on that guy's neck. I'm just about finished, although I'm not positive I've drawn it to the exact, when my phone rings.

I don't bother putting the pencil down—too in the zone —and answer the call without looking at the screen.

"Hello?"

"Hey," Blaine says hesitantly.

I stop drawing and set down the pencil, wariness flooding my body. "Why are you calling me?"

"I just wanted to call and see how you're doing since we haven't talked in a few days." He gives a short pause. "Have you talked to West today?"

I recline against the headboard. "Yeah, he left my house, like, an hour ago."

"Oh." He settles into silence, leaving me to wonder why the hell he's calling.

Just to talk? Or is there more to it? Like, say, he's calling because our blackmailer is making him.

"Did you need anything else?" I ask impatiently.

"No … Yes … I don't know …" He sighs exasperatedly. "I just wanted to tell you that I'm sorry … that I wish things could've been different … and I'm not the guy you think I am. At least, lately I haven't been. And I'm so sorry for hurting you. I really am. It's one of the things I'll always regret the most. And … And I … I love you."

The line clicks.

"H-hello?" My voice is trembling almost as badly as my body. But, what the hell? Why did he say all those things? That he was sorry? That he wasn't the guy I thought he was?

That he … loves me?

It has to be because of the blackmailer. It has to be. Still, I can't shake the sound of his voice, the hint of fear and panic in it.

I try to call him back, but it goes straight to voicemail. Unsure of what else to do, I call West. His doesn't even ring, going straight to voicemail, too, which leaves me wondering if he has his phone turned off. But what?

Unsure of what else to do, I send both of them a text then pace my room as I wait for them to respond. Eventually, Blaine does.

Blaine: I'm fine. I'm sorry for calling you. I was drunk and being an idiot.

I relax a droplet that he at least messaged me back, but … since when does Blaine drink on weekdays? I mean, he's not a saint, but he's also not the kind of guy who'd get hammered on a school night. His dad's a cop, too, so he's usually careful about drinking.

Me: Why are you drinking on a school night?

Blaine: My friends and I were hanging out, and I … well, like I said, I haven't been myself lately.

I may have been pissed off at him, but after what West told me, I feel sort of sorry for him. Am I irritated he didn't tell me what's going on? Yeah. But I also haven't told him a lot of things either.

Me: You want to talk about it? And I mean for real, where we have a two-sided conversation and you don't hang up on me?

Blaine: That sounds nice. How about tomorrow? I think I'm too drunk right now to have that conversation.

Me: Sure. Let's meet up after school.

Blaine: Thanks, Lexi. You really are a good friend.

He must be super drunk since he called me Lexi and hardly anyone ever does.

Me: You know it.

I put my phone down and wait a few more minutes for West to message me back, telling myself that I don't need to feel guilty about spending time with Blaine tomorrow. We're just friends. Nothing more. And I plan on telling West I'm meeting up with him.

However, guilt churns in my stomach, which is so freakin' annoying.

I lie down in bed and turn off my lamp, keeping my phone beside my head, watching the screen, waiting for it to light up with a message from West.

It never does.

I ended up falling asleep with a bad feeling churning in the pit of my stomach.

12

WEST

I messed up.

I screwed up.

I'm so screwed.

These thoughts keep streaming through my head as I sit at the table with Holden, Ellis, and a group of the most sketchiest guys I've ever seen. One of them has arms bulkier than my body while another one is sporting brass knuckles. And don't even get me started on the guy Holden is chatting with. He's the scariest-looking one of all with a knife laying on the table in front of him.

But the conversation they're having is what's unsettling me the most.

"Yeah, we can push that," Holden tells him as he thrums his fingers against the table.

We're in a kitchen of a home that looks a little nicer

than the one I'm currently living in, but not by much. The air smells stale and muggy, and I don't even want to know why. On top of that, I don't really think anyone lives here, since the table is basically the only piece of furniture around, which makes me question what this house is. A place to set up drug trafficking deals? From the conversation going on between Holden and the guys, it probably is.

My phone is turned off due to Holden telling me I had to, and it's making me unsettled. What if something happens to Lex while I'm here and she can't get ahold of me? Would it even matter anyway? Because I feel like, if I try to walk out of here, that knife might end up in my back.

"Good, good," the guy says, his gaze sweeping across Ellis and me. "You guys good with that, too?" he directs his question to Holden.

I want to interrupt. I want to shout "*No!*" Want to say I don't even want to be here. But Holden stressed that neither Ellis nor I should talk while we're here unless directly spoken to, and considering the guys are armed ...

"Yeah, they're good," Holden assures him with his arms crossed.

The guy nods, picks up his knife, and then smooths the pad of his thumb along the blade. "How about we cut a line and seal the deal then?"

Awesome. Now, on top of dealing, I have to do a line? It's not like I haven't done drugs before, but I've been trying to cut back, trying to keep a clear head. For myself. For Lex.

She needs me to be able to keep my shit together.

As everyone does a line, I try to sit back and pretend I'm not here. Eventually, though, the guys start to notice.

"You gotta a problem with my drugs?" the guy who's been doing all the talking asks me.

I want to say yes, but again, my lips remain sealed.

Holden discreetly elbows me hard in the side, and I wince. He gives me the hardest look, warning me that if I mess this up, he'll mess me up.

So, with my jaw ticking, I lower my head and snort a line. And in that moment, I hate myself. I hate my fake parents. I hate that I got into this mess to begin with …

Then that drip trickles down my throat and all that hate sort of blends away.

Everything does. Except regret.

Lots and lots of fucking regret.

13

ALEXIS

I wake up the next morning to my phone buzzing and buzzing and buzzing. At first, I ignore it, but as the sleepiness evaporates from my brain, I realize it might be West.

Nope, just Masie messaging me relentlessly.

Masie: I need to talk to you.

Masie: Please answer

Masie: This is bigger than our fight.

Masie: Lex, please.

Masie: Blaine is gone.

I quickly sit up in bed. "What the hell is she talking about?"

My phone rings then, a call from Masie. Normally, I wouldn't answer it, but something about the way she's texting me has me …

"Hello?" I answer.

"Oh my God, Lex. He's gone! He's just gone!" she shouts into the phone, sobbing and veering toward hysterical.

"Calm down," I say, trying to calm down myself. "What do you mean, *he's gone*? Blaine? What happened?"

"I don't know what happened exactly," she whispers shakily. "Stella, she called me this morning ... She saw on the news ..." She starts crying again. "Blaine's car was found in the lake this morning. He wasn't in it, but the police are searching the lake for him, because they think he's dead."

Blaine is dead?

"No ... There's no way ..." My mind drifts back to the call and messages I received from his last night.

He seemed off and sounded strange—

A messages buzzes through.

"Hold on just a sec," I tell Masie then glance at the message.

It's from *Unknown*.

Dread pinches the pit of my stomach. "Masie ... I have to call you back."

I hang up before she can respond and, with trembling fingers, I open the text.

That dread builds as I see a video attachment, and even though I don't want to, I press *play*.

The video starts with Blaine and West fighting.

This must have been recorded yesterday.

Then the video shifts to Blaine getting into West's car. Then it changes over to them parked in the woods and sitting in the car.

All of this West told me happened yesterday, but the video isn't done yet. It contains one more scene of Blaine's car driving into the lake. Someone is standing on the shore, watching it happen, but it's at night and too dark to see their face.

A message pops through.

Unknown: Look at what West did.

Me: West didn't do that.

Unknown: You sure about that?

Another clip pops through of West sitting in a house and talking to some sketchy-looking men, along with Holden and Ellis.

The person taking the video is clearly peeking in the window, and there's no sound, but I get the gist of what's going on as I watch the men put cocaine on the table. Then everyone snorts lines, including West. At the end, Holden, Ellis, and West carry out bags that I'm guessing have drugs in them.

What is this?

Why is West dealing drugs?

Me: This doesn't prove West put Blaine's car in the lake. He doesn't even have a reason to. You're the one who's blackmailing Blaine and me and taking all these videos.

Unknown: Now Alexis, that's not how we play this game. You don't get to accuse me of anything. Besides, you're the one who's guilty.

Me: The stuff I'm guilty of is mild compared to ... whatever you've done to Blaine.

Unknown: I haven't done anything to him yet, and I won't as long as you play the game correctly.

Me: What damn game?

Unknown: The game where you find the guy you wish was your lover. It's actually a pretty simple game. I give you clues, and if you solve them, you'll find Blaine. You have a week to do it.

Me: And what if I can't find him?

Unknown: Then everyone loses.

I grit my teeth from side to side until my jaw pops. This is such bullshit. I just need to go to the cops.

Unknown: And don't even think of going to the police. Remember the dirt I have on you. On West. Think about what happened in the alley. How easy it was for us to get to you. How easy it is for us to watch you. We'll know if you go to the police, and the moment you do, you'll lose the game. And so will Blaine.

That dread I've felt since I saw the messages from Masie this morning spreads and nausea rises inside me. I swallow down the urge to vomit, though, and try to focus on fixing this.

Us? They've thrown out a hint, I think, without meaning to.

This is more than one person.

It kind of makes sense. With everything that's happened, all the videos taken …

But, just when I think I'm getting somewhere, another video pings through.

Shaking my head in frustration, I push *play*.

Nothing could prepare me for what I see.

Because the video is of my parents, burying something that looks a lot like a body. They're in the middle of the forest, it's late, but the headlights of a vehicle shine on their faces, so I know it's them.

My chest constricts, both panic and anger pounding through me.

Me: This video is edited.

Unknown: Think what you want. It's not.

Me: Go to hell!

Unknown: Tsk. Tsk. That's no way to talk to someone who has enough dirt to destroy everyone in your life. Now go to school and act like the good girl you've been pretending to be lately. But before you leave, look in the top nightstand of your drawer. I left your first clue there.

Vomit burns in my throat as I reach over and open the drawer. Lying inside is a photo of what looks like room located in a basement. In the middle of the room is a chair and on the chair is...

I swallow hard.

Blaine's letterman jacket.

I flip over the photo and on the back is written: *you want to find Blaine, figure out where this is.*

My mind is racing a million miles a minute as I try to figure out how this photo got into the drawer. Then it dawns on me. The power briefly flickered on and off yesterday. Whenever we have power shortage, the house alarm turns off for a few seconds before switching over to the backup battery. But that barely leaves someone enough time to get into the house. Still, if they moved quickly enough, they might be able to get in. But what about getting out?

This doesn't make any sense. Well, unless this person is either smart enough to shut down the house alarm or they know the code.

Panic rushes through me and I have to focus on breathing or else I'm going to have a panic attack.

Air in. Air out. Air in. Air out. Air in. Air out.

As my heart rate settles down, I look at the photo of my parents again.

This can't be real. This person is lying.

My parents didn't bury a body in the middle of the woods.

The video has to be edited.

It has to be.

Still, in the midst of my panic, I start saving the videos, knowing that this blackmailer might erase all the message. And I begin taking screenshots of the messages too. But they only give me time to save one video—the one of my parents—and only one screenshot—the one that basically said West did this to Blaine, so it's not very useful.

From now on, I need to take screenshots as they text me. I make a mental note to do that and also find a way to make this house safer since this person seems to be able to get in and out of it. Then I set down the phone and drag my fingers through my hair.

I want to scream. I want to tell them to go to hell. I want to say I won't play. But deep down, I know I don't have a choice.

Needing to talk to someone, I call West. He doesn't answer and, moments later, sends me a text.

West: Hey, something came up this morning, and I can't make it to school. Sorry I can't drive you, but I'll talk to you soon, okay?

Me: What came up?

West: Just some stuff.

Wow, talk about vague. I can't help thinking that perhaps this has to do with what I saw on the video. Not the part with Blaine, but with the drugs.

It annoys me that he won't be straight with me, but I

guess I should've known better. Everyone lies. Blaine, Masie, me. *My parents.*

I look down at my phone, at the file icon.

What did they do?

I'm not sure, but I'm going to figure it out.

And I'm going to save Blaine.

I'm going to play this game and win, no matter what it takes.

Dear Reader!

Thanks for reading Signed with a Kiss: Accepting the Deal (Alexis Honeyton, #1). Please note that this is a serial series that follows the life of Alexis. There are also stories available that follow the lives of her siblings, so make sure to check those out.

Thanks for reading!
Jessica Sorensen

ABOUT THE AUTHOR

Jessica Sorensen is a *New York Times* and *USA Today* best-selling author who lives in the snowy mountains of Wyoming. When she's not writing, she spends her time reading and hanging out with her family.

ALSO BY JESSICA SORENSEN

<u>Signed with a Kiss Series (Honeyton Alexis):</u>

Accepting the Deal

The Start of a Mysterious Mystery

A Truthful Kiss

Untitled (coming soon)

<u>Rebels & Misfits:</u>

Confessions of a Kleptomaniac

Rules of a Rebels & a Shy Girl

Forget Me Not

Untitled (coming soon)

<u>Enchanted Chaos Series:</u>

Enchanted Chaos

Shimmering Chaos

Iridescent Chaos

Untitled (coming soon)

The Breathing Undead Series:

Breathing Lies

Shadowed Whisperers (coming soon)

My Cursed Superhero Life:

Cursed

Untitled (coming soon)

Capturing Magic:

Chasing Wishes

Chasing Magic

Untitled (coming soon)

Chasing the Harlyton Sisters Series:

Chasing Hadley

Falling for Hadley

Holding onto Hadley

Untitled (coming soon)

Tangled Realms:

Forever Violet

Untitled (coming soon)

Curse of the Vampire Queen:

Tempting Raven

Enchanting Raven

Alluring Raven

Untitled (coming soon)

<u>Unraveling You Series:</u>

Unraveling You

Raveling You

Awakening You

Inspiring You

Every Single Breath

Untitled (coming soon)

<u>Unexpected Series:</u>

The Unexpected Complications of Revenge

Untitled (coming soon)

<u>Shadow Cove Series:</u>

What Lies in the Darkness

What Lies in the Dark

Untitled (coming soon)

<u>Mystic Willow Bay Series:</u>

The Secret Life of a Witch

Broken Magic

Stolen Kisses

One Wild, Crazy, Zombie Night

Magical Whispers & the Undead

Untitled (coming soon)

<u>**Sunnyvale Series:**</u>

The Year I Became Isabella Anders

The Year of Falling in Love

The Year of Second Chances

Untitled (coming soon)

The Coincidence Series:

The Coincidence of Callie and Kayden

The Redemption of Callie and Kayden

The Destiny of Violet and Luke

The Probability of Violet and Luke

The Certainty of Violet and Luke

The Resolution of Callie and Kayden

Seth & Greyson

The Evermore of Callie & Kayden

Untitled (coming soon)

The Secret Series:

The Prelude of Ella and Micha

The Secret of Ella and Micha

The Forever of Ella and Micha

The Temptation of Lila and Ethan

The Ever After of Ella and Micha

Lila and Ethan: Forever and Always

Untitled (coming soon)

Ella and Micha: Infinitely and Always

The Shattered Promises Series:

Shattered Promises

Fractured Souls

Unbroken

Broken Visions

Scattered Ashes

Breaking Nova Series:

Breaking Nova

Saving Quinton

Delilah: The Making of Red

Nova and Quinton: No Regrets

Tristan: Finding Hope

Wreck Me

Ruin Me

The Fallen Star Series:

The Fallen Star

The Underworld

The Vision

The Promise

The Lost Soul

The Evanescence

The Mist of Stars (untitled)

The Darkness Falls Series:

Darkness Falls

Darkness Breaks

Darkness Fades

The Death Collectors Series (NA and YA):

Ember X and Ember

Cinder X and Cinder

Spark X and Spark

Unbeautiful Series:

Unbeautiful

Untamed